Taranath Tantrik

AND OTHER TALES FROM THE SUPERNATURAL

Bibhutibhushan

TRANSLATED FROM THE BENGALI
AND WITH AN INTRODUCTION
BY DEVALINA MOOKERJEE

SPEAKING TIGER

SPEAKING TIGER BOOKS LLP
125A, Ground Floor, Shahpur Jat, near Asiad Village,
New Delhi 110049

First published by Speaking Tiger Books 2022

ISBN: 978-93-5447-364-7
eISBN: 978-93-5447-366-1

10 9 8 7 6 5 4 3 2 1

Typeset in Adobe Garamond Pro by SŪRYA, New Delhi
Printed at ...

Bibhutibhushan Bandyopadhyay (1894–1950) is regarded as one of the greatest Bengali writers. His best known works are the autobiographical novel, *Pather Panchali* (*The Song of the Road*), which was made into a film by Satyajit Ray, *Chander Pahar*, and *Aranyak*.

Devalina Mookerjee is a translator and publisher. She is also a researcher in health and education. Her interest in ghosts is based on two decades of social science research.

She learned to play bass over the lockdown, mostly jazz, blues and folk, and finds that the sound of the bass goes beautifully with stories of ghosts.

She lives in New Delhi with her partner and five dogs.

*

This book is dedicated to Ma, Amma, and Boromashi (Shanta Mookerjee, Chua Chakravarty, and Shukla Hazra) who taught me, in their different ways, how very important it is to have a narrative of my own.

*

CONTENTS

Introduction

Darkness, Karma, and How the Past Refuses to Make a Dignified Exit

We live surrounded by so much light that we have forgotten what it is like to be in the dark—to have darkness surround us and leave no space for even the smallest ray of light. But it was not always like this. For most of known history, humankind has lived in very close proximity with the dark. Half of each twenty-four-hour cycle has been just one candle flame, or one lantern light away from losing sight.

Over a long period of human understanding, darkness has belonged not just to a lack of vision, but also to the spirit—or more appropriately, the spirits. Darkness rushes in where light steps away. And where there is darkness, there is fear, and there may well be ghosts. How would you know otherwise? It's not like you can see them. They could be anywhere.

But the possibility that ghosts may be all around is not in fact the most fearful thing about darkness, because the dark is also akin to other things that are not ghostly. Those other things may not turn your breath to frost, but they have quite as effective ways to terrify you. This is the darkness of the human spirit, the dark in humankind. Human beings have historically shown very little need of support from the otherworld to behave in perfectly horrible ways with other people. This is the point at which the darkness of the uncanny and the darkness of people converge.

Seen against the background of what people are capable of doing to each other, stories of ghost may be seen as corrective mechanisms in the scales of justice. A person who has been wronged returns to tell their story, perhaps to wreak havoc on their tormentors. A disbeliever sits in a seance for which the medium is clearly not prepared, and chaos ensues. We have a word for this already. We call it karma.

Justice and the Ghost

Understandings of power are quite clear in stories of the supernatural. In most revenant or return narratives, ghosts come back because they were powerless in their lives. Being dead frees them from the rules and borders that grip and restrict their actions in life, up to and including mobility. In such narratives, death grants a freedom to women and other marginalized people, to play out a payback fantasy.

In Bengali ghost stories, women (or those who were formerly women) are particularly interesting parts of such revenge scenarios. They return after death to exact a toll from those who treated them badly in life. But where, in life, they had no voice and little power, they are enormously powerful in the realm of ghost. This karmic function of the folklore of ghost is a kind of wish-fulfilment. When the marginalized tell these stories, they embody a hope that the universe has a sort of corrective mechanism built into the scales of justice, that wrongs will be righted, if not in this life, then the next.

People have always told stories to exemplify theories or understand ideas in their lives. We tell stories about family, identity, events, history. Many of the stories that we tell ourselves have varying degrees of relationship with events as they actually occurred, and more to do with symbolic aspects that we would like to highlight, such as those having to do with perceptions of identity, or place in the world.

The degree of anchoring in strict truth becomes of less import in such narratives, because they are meant to tell of collective understandings of life. So the question is not so much a specific supernatural one—did a woman in white pass under the window late at night, leaving a slight perfume of musk? The question is larger, and more thoroughly human—what happens when you go chasing after things that are not intended for you? What happens when you buy property without truly understanding what was there before? What happens when you acquire power by spiritual means, and use that power for material gain?

Consequences are a key idea in stories of the supernatural. Actions have consequences. Greed has consequences. Entitlement has consequences. Stupidity, or lack of thought has consequences. In many cases, the consequences are the balances in the story. In fact, the classic revenant ghost—the ghost which returns—is most often that consequence. An event of imbalance, which is also often an act of injustice, occurs—someone is violently killed, someone covets what is not theirs to have, someone undercuts a fair process to gain profit for themselves. In these stories, the supernatural features as the element to restore balance in an unbalanced world.

Stories of the uncanny do not address questions of probability, but those of morality. In the realm of everyday probability, it is unlikely that a curse cast by a wronged individual in one generation will impact the members of a family two generations later. In the realm of the supernatural story though, not only can this happen, but it is right and just that it does. In the realm of probability, it is unlikely that a merchant gleefully undercutting his competition in the local market will be made to suffer for it. The self-correcting mechanisms in the realm of the uncanny will not only see that this happens, but that it happens in such a way that all the competition gets a good long look at the payback from the universe. This is the logic of stories of ghost, and it is wish-fulfilment in its own way.

The Past and the Present

But the ghosts that we have created to populate the dark corners of the world, and our minds, are more complex than simply embodiments of karmic payback. The human mind is a devious thing, and very good with the richly textured play of symbols.

This is a good point to ask a pivotal question—do ghosts actually exist? Or are they entirely fragments of our imaginations? This is far too weighty a question for me, so I point you to Voltaire. Voltaire claimed that if god did not exist, human beings would find it necessary to invent one. The same may be said of ghosts. If ghosts did not exist, we would have to invent them. We would need to invent them to represent our darkness, and our hopes of justice, yes, but we would also need to invent them because we need a socially acceptable understanding for the very important idea that the past rarely moves on and disappears.

It hangs around our lives, and looks over our shoulders as we try to make decisions, forge relationships, and walk towards the future. Fragments of the past habitually intrude on the present, and they do not need to have a filmy ectoplasmic presence. Time is not linear, a neat straight line running from the past, through the present, into the future, with no point of that line ever touching any other point. In human experience, time is more like a kitten with a ball of string. There's no calculating which part of the string will touch, knot up with, or rip up, which other part. Our lives are but playthings for the universal kitten.

Ghost, in Bengali, is called *bhut*. The past is also called *bhut*. So not only are ghosts and the past perceived as close to one another in the Bengali cultural imagination, they are virtually identical. And since it is unarguable that the past impinges on both the present and the future, the ghosts of the past do not merely peer over our shoulders as we walk into the future. Some are already there, waiting for us.

The Ghosts of Bengal

Bengal has had a long and energetic relationship with ghostkind.

The ghosts of Bengal are multiple and varied in provenance, nature and purpose. They may be missing heads (skandakata), or lying in wait to mislead unwary travellers in the delta marshes of the Sundarbans in Southern Bengal (aleya). The Sundarbans are also populated by the begho bhut, the ghosts of those killed by its tigers. The function of a begho bhut or tiger ghost, is to ensure that others suffer the same death.

Ghosts in Bengal may live in banyan, tamarind or peepul trees (gecho bhut), or bamboo-groves (besho bhut), and have the reputation of wanting to give passers-by horribly painful wedgies.

Ghosts specializing in fish (mecho bhut) may steal fish from kitchens or ponds. If you're missing anything other than fish, a chorachunni may be responsible. These are the ghosts of thieves, and they act more out of habit of mischief than malignancy.

Social division persists beyond death, with Brahmin ghosts, who are by and large mean, short-tempered, and thin-skinned, called brahmadatti, and Muslim ghosts called mamdo.

If a nishi bhut sets its target on you, it will call your name three times in the dead of night, in the voice of someone you know. If you answer, or even worse, get up and leave the room to respond to the call, you may never be heard of again. The jokkha, or jokh, guards treasure, and there are rituals through which a powerful or rich living human being may set such a supernatural guard. But the price of such a setting, as with all human-supernatural arrangements, is high. This aspect of ghostkind—the possibility of human-supernatural understandings leading to benefit, or not, as the case may be, for the human in the arrangement—is a doorway to the other liminal realm that adjoins it, the realm of the tantras. There is a short note about tantra before the first Taranath Tantrik story, please look at it for more details.

Some shapeshifters are called damabanu. If you're travelling across the countryside and come across a group of lovely maidens holding hands and dancing in the dead of night, they're probably damabanu. It may be wise to keep away. The pechapechi takes the form of an owl, and will follow you until you are alone and properly vulnerable. Then it will descend from the trees and feed on your blood. If you get up from a bad dream paralysed with fear, and find that you can't move, that's because a boba bhut is sitting on your chest.

Female ghosts may be married (shakchunni), or unmarried (petni). Both have an unpleasant propensity to strangle people, but the petni in particular longs to have a husband and a marital home, and will occasionally strangle for this purpose. You can tell them apart because the shakchunni wears a shakhas or shell bangles, which are a symbol of marriage in Bengal and are broken at widowhood. A petni's wrists may well be bare.

(Note that the names of ghost categories in this section are from the demotic Bengali, and not the Sanskrit roots.)

Bengali Ghosts and the World

While many of these ghosts are culturally specific—it is improbable that a culture less fish-loving would devote a ghost to the purpose—several common Bengali ghosts have echoes around the world.

The aleya of the Sundarbans is a light in the marshes that leads travellers to believe that shelter may be found ahead. Such bioluminescence, which is created by the action of methane and decaying organic matter, is found in waterways around the world. English folklore tells you not to follow the will o' the wisp. They inscribed the idea of an unknown light that you follow to your peril, and made a literary trope out of it. Finnish folklore talks of the virvatuli, which has a creation myth remarkably like the aleya of the Sundarbans, and a spin that makes them possible keepers of treasure—a characteristic shared by werelights in Mexico, and the jokkho of Bengal.

In parts of Argentina, Uruguay, and Paraguay, the luz mala or evil light populate stories with examples of what not to do if you're walking in the dark and there are unknown lights in the distance.

The Bengali kandhakata has a parallel in New England, where Washington Irving's 1929 story, 'The Legend of Sleepy Hollow' drew both on local legends of a headless horseman and on much older German folktales. The penchapechi corresponds to the vampire of European folklore, except with the owl as a vehicle, not bats or rats. The boba bhut is otherwise described as the night hag phenomenon, or sleep paralysis, and appears to unfortunate sleepers around the world. This ghost has a rather telling depiction in Enlightenment art—Henry Fuseli's 'The Nightmare', first exhibited in 1782.

The Japanese onryo is a female ghost that was abused by a lover and stays in the realm of the living to seek revenge. Like the female ghosts of Bengal, onryo have a great deal more power than the women they were when alive. Sailor ghosts, like the Japanese funayurei, appear in a story in this collection, with some of the stories around such ghosts showing remarkable similarity across Japan and Bengal.

There are more contemporary readings of ghost in Western writing, of which a favourite is from Ben Aaronovich's *Rivers of London* series. As hypothesized by Peter Grant, paranormal detective-constable working with the Metropolitan Police, ghosts arise from the intersections between personalities and objects. A personality gets stamped on a physical object, and remains associated with that object beyond death. Aaronovich calls this vestigia. This present volume has a Bibhutibhushan story about vestigia, featuring an ancient monk who imprinted on an object he loved.

Death and the Living

Human beings have two moments of truly universal experience in their lifetimes. The first is birth. The annals of both folklore and literature are full of narratives, understandings and framings of birth, through individual or collective memory.

The other moment is death, and this too has its stories and interpretations. Death is considered the greatest and last mystery, and centuries of thought and lengthy discussion has brought human beings little actual understanding of what, if anything, follows it.

Our ancestors could have told us that death was fundamentally unknowable. They addressed the what-lies-after question by creating an understanding of a kind of continued life after death, a life that included social functions and effectiveness, and designated it the realm of ghosts. In an act of sophisticated reconciliation with the notion of rebirth, they designated unfinished business as the filter. If you have unfinished business, take the fork in the road to ghosthood, if not, proceed ahead to rebirth.

The actions of ghostkind are interesting in that they

illuminate not just human understandings of death, but also human understandings of life, decisions, behaviour and consequences. This is exactly how ghosts work in the realm of folklore, that, in many cultures, eventually finds its way into literature though prolonged and repeated exposure in the realm of oral storytelling.

Ghost stories, or, to widen the category, stories of the supernatural or the uncanny, provide frames of understanding about the people and the folk wisdoms that tell these stories—the people who symbolically imbue with meaning, themselves, and their views of the world. Once you've finished looking at the story, goes the saying, don't forget to take a good long look at the teller. Look at the collective mind that constructed such actions, and such consequences. Look at the world that birthed these notions of attachment and its border with control. Look at the living hivemind that passed them around in louder and louder whispers until they were loud enough to be written down.

From the Oral to the Written

Perhaps one of the most important points to be made here is that not all supernatural stories that are told, survive. Most supernatural stories begin as oral narratives, in the realm of the telling of an event, and are passed around by word of mouth as rumour. Warnings about that desolate lake, or that path which passes through a dense patch of bamboo, or those particular nights it is best to stay in, are passed around and become stronger stories as they are told and retold.

Folktale research tells us that the survival of stories—which depends on whether stories will be repeated—depends on how, and how much, the story echoes with the understandings of the world of the communities in which these stories are told. Stories that reflect such understandings are repeated until they become a part of the lore of that place, and people start warning others to stay away from that bamboo grove, that lake, to mark the calendar and stay in on certain nights. So are hauntings and other supernatural occurrences established in local folklore.

Some of these stories, the ones which have been repeated often and so grown strong, find their way to the written form. Let us consider the legend of the black dog. In Munger, Bihar, of the 1950s, night sightings of a large, ghostly black dog were reported by several people around the town. Nobody knew where it came from, or where it went in the day. It was an astonishingly large dog, black as night, and some said its enormous eyes gleamed red in the darkness. Seeing it meant being frightened witless, and possible illness, with the additional burden of bad luck for the person.

The writer Saradindu Bandyopadhyay, creator of the Bengali detective Byomkesh, lived in Munger at the time. He wrote a supernatural story about this black dog, so codifying it, and moving it into the realm of Bengali literature. Some of the numerous supernatural black dog stories of the British Isles have been codified and moved into literature in the same way. The most famous of these is Conan Doyle's *Hound of the Baskervilles*, but there are more, including a recent appearance in Andrew Cartmel's *Vinyl Detective* series. The literature of the supernatural has strong foundations in folklore, and folklore is always an expression of the understanding of a culture of itself, transforming and adapting, as forms of cultural understanding and expression change.

Stories of the uncanny change and adapt as cultures and contexts change. An example of this is the woman-in-white, waiting-on-the-path theme, ubiquitous in Indian ghost folklore. When these stories were originally told, the woman in white was to be found waiting at bends in forest paths, or deserted parts of large properties. She still waits, but now on roads and quiet bylanes. Similarly, older stories focused on haunted objects like oil lamps, which evolved through lanterns, and torches, and electric bulbs. The ghosts that used to haunt crumbling mansions now rattle the doors of urban apartments. The frames and structures of stories survive. But as cultural contexts evolve, so does oral folklore, and its dependent written form.

The question, then, is not if ghosts do or do not exist. The question is, why do we tell these stories? Why do we keep telling them over and over again, until the narrative groove is worn so deep that they find their way into writing?

We do this because supernatural stories resonate with peoples' understandings of how the world works.

Relationships, gender, status, food, power, memory, desire, belief, wish-fulfilment, all the powerful forces that drive human existence and co-existence, are the drivers of these stories. An example of this is the mecho bhut (ghost of fish), a figure at the intersection of gender, status, food, and desire. If a certain number of pieces of fish have been cooked in a kitchen, and several are found to have gone missing when the dish is served, a mecho bhut is to blame. It is greedy for fish, and roams kitchens looking for fish to steal and eat.

Look back in time at the world in which such stories were told, and the story runs deeper. Traditional gender norms dictated that men ate first, and got the best pieces of fish. Where there was plenty of food, women would get some fish too, but very often women would be left with the less-desirable, high-bone pieces, or no fish at all. Would it be difficult to imagine that women in kitchens around Bengal became tired of this situation, and helped themselves to the delicacy before the dish was served to the men in the family? From this perspective, the ghost of fish is not just a story about ghosts, fish, or even food. It is a story about men and women, their relationships, power, subversion, agency, and desire. That these stories also draw explanations from locations in the aftermath of death marks them as culturally significant, and lends to them a light that some may call unreal, and others may call truth.

Justice and Social Dis/order in the Supernatural Stories of Bibhutibhushan

Bibhutibhushan Bandyopadhyay needs no introduction to readers of Bengali, and to those familiar with the movies of Satyajit Ray. Four of Ray's well-known movies—*The Apu Trilogy*, beginning with *Pather Panchali* (Song of the Little Road); and *Ashani Shanket* (Distant Thunder), are based on novels by Bibhutibhushan.

The themes of the stories in this book point to larger understandings about humanity. But the stories themselves are told in the context of the Bengal of Bibhutibhushan's time, which is the first half of the twentieth century. Roughly a century ago, Bengal lived mostly in its villages. It is true that the twin cities of Calcutta and Dhaka (now in Bangladesh) were glittering centres of both indigenous and colonial power. But in the manner of cities in that time, they were for the relatively well-placed, or for those seeking to be relatively well-placed. The vast majority of Bengal did not live in these cities, they lived in villages and towns scattered across undivided Bengal. Some villages were just a handful of houses surrounded by agricultural fields and forests. Some were larger, but almost none had electricity or tap water. Most roads, except those going to larger towns and cities, were not paved. Narrow, unpaved paths ran through villages, and these would become mud for the part of the year around the three months of annual rain. The streams and rivers would overflow onto fields during the monsoon, and fish was plentiful and free when this happened.

Bengal is still green. But a century ago, when nature had a chance against man, her green would have been lush beyond description, a living wild green monstrous overload. It would have been dark on those paths, under those trees, after dusk, much darker than we can imagine today.

For ordinary people, living was hyper-local. The outside world was reachable only by foot, or bullock-cart, which is an exceedingly slow method of transport. In such a world, the ghost living in the banyan tree beside the local pond would be a closer member of the daily functioning community than, say, the younger son of the landlord who left the village for an education long ago and rarely returns. If you were a woman of the village, you knew that the petni in the tree would sit on a branch and dangle her feet down at you, while trying to persuade you to drown yourself so she could replace you in your family. This was upsetting, certainly, but also predictable. Doubtless, generations of women drawing water from the pond close to dusk had ways to refuse such invitations. But a grown man from a much higher social class, a feudal lord, last seen at the age of seven? In the scale of ordinary things, that's a strange situation.

At the other end of the spectrum is the city featured in these stories, Calcutta, now officially called what it has always been in Bengali—Kolkata. A bustling city with roads, trams, vehicles, lights, and bookstores, a further world cannot be imagined from the rural Bengal of the time. The city houses both sceptics and believers, men with money they are willing to give for services, and those who would take the money and provide an uncertain understanding of services rendered. Taranath Tantrik comes to the city to lose his faith, but arguably his faith was already in waiting to be lost. So do our ghosts wait for us, ahead, somewhat hidden by the bend in the road.

The writer of the stories in this book was acutely perceptive about both worlds, of the village, and the city of his time. Much more can and has been said about the extraordinary writing of Bibhutibhushan in his native language, Bengali. But here, for the purposes of introducing his stories of fear, it would be appropriate to focus on his developed ideas of social justice.

The twin notions of empathy and emotion are a good place to begin. Empathy is the ability to identify with suffering—not simply understand it, but to suffer alongside. In Maya, a story translated for this volume, the protagonist is a cook. At the beginning of the story, he has been unfairly accused of stealing from his employers. Sacked for this reason, he is walking away from his accusers, in no pre-decided direction, under the burning sun of midsummer Bengal. The buzzing in his head is a combination of outrage at injustice, resignation, and fear for the future. We know this as readers, because the writer is right there, walking beside him under the raging midsummer sun, suffering with him. We know this as surely as we know the relief he feels when he finds a shaded pond with cool water to take a dip, and how his stomach growls with hunger once his body has cooled off.

For centuries, it was believed that the body of the king indicated the health of the kingdom. In Bibhutibhushan's stories, this construct is transformed to something far more specific and personal—the suffering of the individual. The suffering of the individual indicates the disorder of society, the suffering is the disorder. Moreover, it is not the suffering of kings with which he is concerned, it is with the suffering of the vulnerable, the marginalized, those who have no voice in life. The little girl who feels left behind, the medium who supports her family and so needs to sit in seance whenever a skeptic demands proof, the village woman subject to predation by the powerful landlord, these are the sufferings Bibhutibhushan points to as disorder.

Disorder requires order, and the re-establishment of order in these stories is also the establishing of justice. But this order is imposed on a sliding scale, from the Old-Testament-style wrath of 'the curse', to the opportunity to tell an individual story that needs to be told, in 'the statue'. The act of justice, or re-establishment of order is consonant in intensity with the disorder that called it into being. Abduction and rape are very serious acts of disorder, which require an equally violent balance. But being forgotten by time, that can be rectified by an opportunity to speak in the present.

The two Taranath Tantrik stories translated for this

volume take these ideas to a different, altogether more subtle territory. Taranath Tantrik is a failed godman, for practical purposes, a fake. It is clear that Bibhutibhushan had strong opinions about fake godmen and other illusionists that prey on belief, given his diatribes on the subject in these stories. What makes the character of Taranath both complex and interesting, though, is that he has also been, in the past, a real spiritualist. He has seen the actual thing, and partaken of some measure of authentic tantrik power himself. Then he lost the power he had, not because of any external enemy, but through the workings of his own nature. We watch him repeatedly doing the wrong thing, tripping himself up in any way he can, sliding faster down the rabbit hole, entirely through his own actions. What happens to him is inevitable, a balancing on the scales of order, and it begs the very important question—what happens to human beings when the darkness is within?

Enjoy the stories.

THE TARANATH TANTRIK STORIES

A Note on Tantra

WHAT IS TANTRA?

Tantra is a practice. It is the procedure, method, how-to-do-it end of the goal of transcending the material world, or merging with the godhead. The practice of tantra (or simply practice) requires a guru or a guide, and is done in steps. An important step involves acquiring the ability to call and control supernatural figures of varying power.

Who is a tantrik?

A tantrik is a person who practices tantra as a means of, at the lower level, acquiring skills in the spiritual realm, and at the higher level, becoming indistinguishable from the godhead.

What is tantra discipline?

The discipline of tantra broadly involves meditation, specific chants for specific purposes, and rituals, at least some of which require a human corpse.

Particular combinations of these are aimed towards the acquiring of specific powers via the godheads towards which the practitioner of tantra aims the discipline.

Called sadhana, the discipline of tantra is usually difficult and takes long periods of time.

What is the tantrik attitude to money? Tantra being used to make money?

At the purely practical end, the skills of practitioners are used by people wanting to engage spirits to exorcise or negate other bad spirits, or call on good ones to help them, such as in astrology. It is acceptable to accept money for such services rendered, especially within the Hindu tradition of tantra.

However, the power of tantra is essentially spiritual in nature, and it will be damaged or lost if it is consistently used for gain in the purely material world.

What is the Mahadamori?

An obscure and secretive form of tantrik practice. Very little is known about it in the contemporary world, and practitioners are not popularly known.

The First Story

DUSK WAS BEGINNING to slope towards night. I was looking through old books in an area of bookshops, when my old friend Kishori Sen appeared as if from nowhere and hailed me—'There you are! What are you doing here? Well, since you're here, come with me. Let's go and meet the palmist and show him our hands. You've heard of Taranath the astrologer, of course? He's very well known. People say that he's a man of knowledge.'

I have always enjoyed meeting palmists and astrologers, although, truth to tell, I'd never met one that lived up to their publicity. 'What's a good astrologer?' I asked Kishori, 'Will whatever he says come true? Can he see both my past and my current life? What about the future? Can I believe him if he talks about the future?'

My friend was amused, 'Just come with me,' he said, 'you have some money, right? It'll be two rupees to get a reading. Find out for yourself if you can trust him, or not.'

We entered a nearby narrow lane and walked up to a regular-looking one-storey house which displayed a flimsy tin signboard:

Taranath Astrology
Palms and Horoscopes read here
Amulets harnessing Planetary Strength prepared
in the Tantrik way
Come and See for yourself!
Recommendations from Kings and
Other Important people.
Very Affordable

'We're here,' said Kishori.

I laughed aloud. 'This person is totally bogus. Look at the house! Apparently all these kings and important people revere him, and he lives here?'

Kishori rattled the door-handle, and a child's voice from inside called, 'Who is it?'

'Is the astrologer home?'

There was a short silence. Then the door opened to a small gap. The face of a child we assumed to be a boy appeared in the gap and regarded us with suspicion. After a period of silent scrutiny, the child asked, 'Where are you from?'

We told him why we had come, and he trotted off and disappeared into the house. There was another period of silence.

'I think your astrologer lives in fear of the debts he owes,' I chuckled. 'That's why his doors are locked. He sent the child to find out if we are debtors. I'm sure he'll call us in very soon.' I was proved right in a minute or two. The child returned and opened the door all the way. 'Come in,' he said.

We sat in a small room on a basic wooden cot. Some time later, a door was pushed open and an old gentleman walked into the room. Kishori stood up and greeted him respectfully. I kept sitting, mentally assessing the man.

He was in his early sixties, and extremely fair. His skin had a kind of glow you would expect in a much younger person. The face under an almost entirely bald head was very intelligent—to be more exact, it was clever with a measure of cunning. The prominent jaw indicated firmness and consistency. He had bright, wide-open eyes. I thought of Lord Redding, who had a degree of visual similarity with the man in front of me. But there was one significant difference. Where Lord Redding bore himself with an assured confidence, the lines around this man's eyes betrayed a loss of faith. I thought he looked like the kind of man who had lost a large measure of the self-belief with which he had started out.

I showed my palm first.

He examined my palm closely for a minute, and then looked up at me. 'You were born on the fifteenth of Sravan, in the year thirteen oh five. Right? You got married in thirteen twenty-seven, on the same date. Right? But people don't usually marry in the same month they were born. How did this happen? I'm seeing the month quite clearly, but this is very unusual!'

He was right. I had several reasons to remember the day, among which were memories of loud objections from relatives about the marriage taking place in an anniversary month of my birth. Having never met me before, the astrologer could not possibly have known this. In fact even my friend Kishori Sen had had no occasion to know this because we had met only two years ago at a bridge-players group, in which there was neither any room, nor reason, to discuss such personal matters.

The old man continued, 'You have two sons and one daughter. Your wife is currently quite ill. You fell off a high tree, or almost drowned when you were young, maybe thirteen—whatever it was, you should count yourself lucky for having survived that dangerous time basically unharmed.' He was right on every point. Evidently, the man did have some power. I began to feel a grudging respect for him.

He shifted gear to the present, 'You are currently under some kind of psychological stress. You also seem to have lost money recently. You're not going to get that money back, it's gone. In fact, I see more loss of funds in the near future.'

I stared at him in astonishment. I had lost my wallet with some money in it just two days ago. As far as I could make out, this had happened while I was getting off the tram at Kolutola Street that day. I'd been so embarrassed by the incident that I hadn't even mentioned it at home. Perhaps Taranath had skills in a kind of mind-reading?

But if he was reading my thoughts, how would he know that there was more loss of money coming up in the future? That part was probably made up. But even if he had made the last part up, it was evident that his purpose in inventing predictions was not to make his client happy. This, in itself, made him different from the usual line of soothsayers that I had encountered.

That evening Taranath told me several other facts about my life. My respect for him grew. I started seeing him occasionally, and not always to have my palm read. I would drop by, and we would sit and talk.

He had a strange history. As he said it, his fascination with spirituality and practitioners of spiritual discipline had started at a young age. He had followed this interest a long time. Over his many associations with monks, priests and godmen, he had met a tantrik teacher with a measure of real power. Taranath had become a disciple, and the teacher had imparted some power to him, taught him a little about the tantrik way. Armed with this beneficence, Taranath had come to Kolkata and found ways to make money using the knowledge granted by his spiritual teacher.

He began to specialize in the share market, the horse races, in any kind of speculation in which future outcomes could be predicted for profit. His reputation spread rapidly. Very soon, the area outside his house became crowded with the cars of big businessmen who wanted to seek his advice on matters of investment. Money started to pour in. But the nature of quick and easy money is that it leaves with the same ease that it comes in, and this is exactly what happened.

He had three addictions—the horse races, women,

and alcohol. Trying to keep these three goddesses appeased had ruined so many men of far greater and more entrenched wealth, and Taranath was, after all, only a simple predictor of numbers. He made a lot of money over his first few years in Kolkata, but the next few years were his undoing. All the money evaporated into the ether like camphor left carelessly out in the open air. There was also the additional and very important factor of his supernatural spiritual abilities, which did not stand up well to repeated use for reasons of pure profit. His abilities, too, began to wane and soon deserted him almost entirely.

As his abilities dwindled, they took with them his reputation on the market. Taranath had to use all the cleverness, strategy, and business-sense at his disposal to prevent himself from going under. He survived and, miraculously, preserved what turned out to be a small degree of ability, and a fraction of his former reputation.

At the time we met, Taranath's foremost preoccupation was with dodging his debts. The practice of tantra, and even lower-grade prediction, had been relegated to the category of things he no longer had very much time for. It was clear, however, that as someone who was interested in his skills, I was a valuable rarity in his life. Not many people trusted him or his powers anymore, so my belief was like a support to him, a glimpse of a way to return to self-belief. We became friends, of a kind.

He would periodically tell me, 'I'll teach you everything. You will be my last and only student. Through you, people will see if Taranath has real powers or not. I had lost hope of finding anyone fit to receive the gift of my knowledge, until I met you.'

One day he said, 'Do you know how to perceive the moon? Not just see it, but actually perceive it? I will teach you how to do this. Hold your eyes closed with the fingers of both hands. Then use your thumbs to tightly stop your ears. Lie down flat on your back. Do this for a few days, and you will be able to perceive the moon. It will be right in front of your eyes, a huge full moon. Under it will be a tree, and under that, two beings of pure spirit. They will tell you anything you want to know. Nothing is left unrevealed to those who practise this discipline regularly.'

I did not practise to perceive the moon, but I did see Taranath more or less regularly. He talked of such strange things, topics that were not only unknown and undiscussed among the other people I met, but also ones that seemed to have no contact whatsoever with the banality of the everyday work-and-home routine. I had no idea that such things existed, and that they were discussed in normal conversation, before I met him.

One rainy evening I went to Taranath's house and found him slowly turning the pages of a book, so old that the thick pages had become cottony with use. He saw me and said, 'Let's go to Beleghata, I hear a well-known sage has put up there. Some say he is a great tantrik. Let's have a look at him.'

Taranath regularly kept track of godmen in his

vicinity, particularly if word of mouth said that the individual in question had inclinations towards tantra. When that happened, he would drop everything else and obsessively devote all his time to seeking favour from the tantrik godman.

We went to Beleghata. The godman showed us some small skills, and then asked me to name a smell, any smell. I thought of the fragrance of the wood-apple flower, that some call arabian jasmine. 'Do you have a handkerchief in your pocket?' asked the godman, 'Why don't you take it out and have a look?'

I pulled out my handkerchief and a strong smell of wood-apple flower scented the air. The fragrance was clearly coming from the square of fabric that had been in my pocket. My initials were in the corner, so it had not been exchanged with another one. In any case, nobody had come close enough to effect such an exchange—the only people in the room were the godman, Taranath, and me. Taranath and I were sitting at least six feet from the godman, and at no point had he tried to reduce this distance.

This was interesting, no doubt, but not particularly impressive. I felt that if someone spent the time and effort to walk the difficult, complex path of tantra, even if for only a short while, the results should be grander than a bit of distilled flower essence on a handkerchief. The point of spiritual practice which led to such a minor outcome was lost on me. Everyone knew that distilled essences of all the perfumed flowers were freely available on the market.

On the way back, Taranath agreed with my lukewarm assessment. 'It seems that the man has attained a lower form of power through tantra,' he commented, 'that seems to have given him some few skills. But this is all he knows.'

I found myself rather more impressed as I continued to think the matter over. Looking at the event from a scientific point of view, the man had somehow arranged, from a distance, for the fragrance of a flower to appear in my pocket. Any smell, he had said, and I had named the first one that popped into my head. I could well have named any other. But he had managed to move the physical content of the chosen flower essence, over a distance, and into my pocket. A little pointless, maybe, but these were not skills to be scoffed at.

Perhaps he did it through hypnotism. Hypnotism would explain my smelling the wood-apple flower while I was sitting in front of him. But my handkerchief still had lingering traces of the fragrance in it. Did that mean that the man's skills in hypnotism held constant over a distance? Now that would be a skill to possess!

We returned to Taranath's house. 'I see that you're thinking that the man has some power, but I didn't see a real tantrik,' he said disparagingly. 'The lower orders of tantrism show themselves as a kind of magic. You can call it black magic, because that's all it is. I have also practised that level of tantra in the past. A smell of perfume is nothing compared to the powerful tantriks I have seen. You wouldn't believe me if I told you those stories. I knew a tantrik who would swallow poison, with no ill effects. A man like this came to Kolkata a while ago. He drank sulphuric acid and nitric acid and survived unscathed. Not even a mark on his tongue!

'I've seen greater strength than that, too. There was a very well-known sage in the area in which I grew up, in Bankura. An aunt of mine was his disciple so he used to visit our home quite often. He was very fond of us, the children of the house. Whenever he came home, he always spent at least a part of the time with us. He would often tell us that there's a light in our forehead, a little above the point between our eyes. "Concentrate on the spot," he would say, "If you focus on it hard enough, you will see that light." I had to try for two or three months before I could see the light.'

Listening to Taranath holding forth, it struck me that this could be a concocted story, like the one about perceiving the moon. But I asked him, 'What kind of light did you see?'

***

Taranath began narrating:

'It was the purplish-blue of a bolt of lightning. I had started the meditation quite casually. One late evening, a little before dusk, I went and sat under the guava tree in our back garden. Focusing on the point above my nose—as the godman had asked—I tried to see the light for about an hour. Needless to say, nothing happened. I tried again two or three days later, and about twice a week after that. It became a kind of routine. I'd sit under the tree and try to focus between my brows with as much concentration as I could muster, for about an hour each time. About three months into this practice, I suddenly saw the light on my forehead just as he had promised. It was an intense purplish-blue flame, thin and long, but steady. It stayed about a minute the first time.

I've been attracted to the spiritual, to godmen and sages from the time I was a child. A short while after seeing the blue flame, the everyday life of family and society became increasingly tiresome to me. I broke into the box in which my grandmother kept money and took enough to get me straight to Benaras.

One evening in Benaras, I was sitting by the river on the steps of the Ahalya Bai Ghat. It was not yet dark. I could hear the evening's prayers being offered at a nearby temple. Glancing idly around, I saw a tall, broad-shouldered man dressed in the robes of a sage, wooden sandals on his feet, and the familiar water-pot for ritual offering in his hand, descending the steps towards the river. There was something about the air of the man that attracted me immensely, to the point that I could not look anywhere else because I could not take my eyes off him. I had by then already seen quite a few men of god, but this one felt different.

I waited quietly for him to return. He filled the pot with water from the river and started to climb back up the steps, angling towards my direction. As he got closer, he looked directly at me and said in clear Bengali, "And where is the young gentleman from?"

"District Bankura, Maliyara Rudrapur," I replied.

He stopped abruptly. "Maliyara Rudrapur?" He said quietly. Then he was silent, as if preoccupied with something that was visible only to his mind's eye. The reverie broke in a few beats, and he looked at me as if he saw me again.

"Have you heard of Ramrup Sanyal of Rudrapur?" he asked. "Do you know anyone in that family?"

I knew that sometime in the past, the Sanyal family of our village had been very wealthy. Local legend said that they used to have a huge house, with elephants—notoriously expensive and hard to maintain—tethered in their yard. But that was a long time ago. The glory days of the Sanyals was now a thing of the distant past. I had never heard of a Ramrup Sanyal.

I told the sage as much, and he laughed. "Of course you wouldn't have, you're so young," he said, "But that is as it should be. I hope the Shiva temple still stands near the ferry?"

I'd never heard of a ferry. There was no longer even a river at Rudrapur, it had dried up a long time ago, the dry riverbed had become a walkway for people and animals. But there was an old, broken-down temple on what may have been a higher part of the bank of the river, near the village. I had seen it as chunks of rock, brick and rubble, the few standing structures impenetrably festooned in encroaching green. Local lore said that a Sanyal ancestor had established that temple a long time ago. But how did this sage on the river-steps in Benaras know that history?

"You know a lot about our village!" I said, my tone betraying my surprise. He smiled a small, sweet smile, almost to himself. It was the kind of smile a grandfather may direct at a young and mistaken, but much loved grandchild—perhaps in response to something naive the child has said. I still remember that smile, and have a clear memory of thinking that a human being truly needs to have transcended earthly matters in some way, in order to be able to smile that particular kind of smile.

"Why have you left home?" He asked, in a gentle voice that also held a question. "Are you looking for a life of faith?" I did not reply, and he didn't wait for an answer. "Go back home," he said, "be with your family, in your world. Listen to me when I say that this path is not for you."

"That's very cruel!" I burst out. "How can you say that? Why shouldn't this life be right for me? I don't want to be with my family and their world. That's why I left!"

He laughed briefly. "That's not what is called leaving the world. You haven't left any world, nor will you be able to. I can see that you're young, perhaps you didn't think this over enough. Don't hurt your parents any more. Go back home."

He said this with an air of finality and turned to

leave. I tried to stop him. "You didn't tell me how you know so much about our village! Please tell me that before you go?"

By now he was briskly walking away. I ran after him, undeterred. He walked on for a while, then turned around. "Why are you following me?"

I had made up my mind. "I'm not going to let you be," I said. "I don't want anything from you, just to stay by your side."

"You won't gain anything from being by my side," in that gentle, grandfatherly voice I'd heard before, "you have to have a life in your world. Your capacity is for that world, not this one. Go away, go back there. You have my blessings, they will ensure your success in that world."

He walked away, and I could not follow him anymore. I mean that literally, I could not follow him because it was as if a block or some physical force kept me from moving forward. My vision misted over. When it cleared and I could step forward again, the man had disappeared into Benaras's innumerable narrow winding streets, there was no sign of him that I could see.'

Taranath paused for a few moments, then continued.

'I must take a minute to finish this particular story. Many years after this incident, I was back at home and asked around among the oldest people in my village, those whose memories would be likely to go back a long way. Nobody had any memory, however distant, of Ramrup Sanyal. It seemed that all the younger people in that family had left the village a while ago.

I eventually found one man, a distant relative of the family, who had spent most of his life as a post-office worker at Jalpaiguri. He visited the village a few winters after he retired. We met one day, and I asked him the same questions. He was somewhat bemused at my curiosity, but more helpful than anyone else had been so far. "When I was quite young, my father's oldest brother had a book," he said. "It was written by hand, a kind of record of the history of our family. Family genealogy was his personal interest. I knew that he had gone through all kinds of trouble and done years of research on our family, much of it on foot, to add to that book. I heard from him that four or five generations before mine, an ancestor called Ramrup Sanyal built that temple on the riverbank. He was a spiritual kind of man, aloof from the material world, never married, had no children. Ramrup apparently had an older brother called Ramnidhi. That man was of a very strong spiritual and religious bent. He left home as quite a young man, and never returned. But we're talking of events that took place between a hundred to a hundred and fifty years ago."'

'About that Shiva temple Ramrup Sanyal built,' I interjected before Taranath could continue, 'why did he build it at such an awkward spot, away from the regular paths of local devotees?'

'That he didn't do,' said Taranath. 'The man told me that Ramrup built it right beside the path that almost anyone in the village would have to take to the river. The water flowed wide and deep at that time, in fact, that part of the river yielded a lot of taxes from boats passing through. Sometime in the past, a boat had capsized near a point on the riverbank just below the temple, so everyone knew that pier of the ferry service as the Boat-breaker Ferry.

I heard the word from the man, and almost shrieked it back at him—Ferry?! Understandably, he was somewhat taken aback at this disproportionate response. I think he took it for disbelief, because he hurriedly responded, "Yes, yes, I have heard from my father's older brother that there was a ferry at that spot. Besides, I think we still may have the old papers stating that a Shiva temple was built by the family, just above the Boat-breaker Ferry. But why are you asking all these questions? Are you planning to write a book?"

I didn't tell anyone at the time, but I started to believe then that the man I had met at the Ahalya Bai Ghat at Benaras was Ramrup Sanyal's elder brother, Ramnidhi. That belief persists till this day. I think he found some yogic remedy to the process of ageing, and managed to live, hale and hearty, till the age of a hundred and fifty—or more, for all I know.

I did not last too long at home, in my world. Leaving home and the village again, I went in search of someone who would direct my way on a spiritual path. The many enquiries I had made led me to a particular cremation-ground beside a river in the district of Birbhum. Rumour had it that a madwoman of incredible tantrik powers was to be found there.

I went to meet her. She was sitting on the bare ground, wrapped in a dirty old quilt that was beginning to fall apart. Dirt caked her face and limbs, and her dreadlocks were frightful to look at, if only for the filth they seemed to harbour. She got extremely annoyed at me for showing up on her territory. "Get out!" she growled, by way of greeting, "Who told you to come and bother me here?"

My first reaction to the disordered, mean, filthy mess in front of me was revulsion. But I had heard that the woman had remarkable powers, so I swallowed that instinctive response and kept my focus on longer-term goals.

"Mother, I implore you, take me as your devotee and student. I've travelled very far to come to you. Have mercy on me!"

"Get out right now," she yelled, "You'll be in trouble if you stay! Go!" She pointed towards the path to the village.

The cremation ground was desolate, quite far away from the nearest houses. I felt afraid. She looked so angry, close to the borderline with violent. She was also, clearly, insane. Such people are capable of anything at any time. Considering all this I decided not to prolong the conversation and quietly slunk away from the cremation ground and the madwoman in it.

But something about the outlandish figure intrigued me enough to overcome the fear. I went back to the cremation ground the next evening.

"Why are you back?" demanded the madwoman.

"Mother, I beg you—"

"Go away! Just leave, go anywhere, get out from here!" Then, to my utter shock, she kicked me, quite hard. She was yelling, "I'm warning you, you'll regret it if you dare to come here again!"

That night I lay in bed and thought that it was time to leave that place. The madwoman may try to kill me if she saw me again, and I had no other reason to be there.

I had a vivid dream in the very early hours of the next morning. The madwoman came to me in the dream. But she was no longer even mildly annoyed, in fact she was looking benign and sympathetic. "You poor thing, you got hurt when I kicked you," she smiled gently, "Now, don't feel bad anymore, come and see me tomorrow."

I rushed to see her the next morning. But it turned out to be a false dream, because she got very angry when she saw me. In her rage, she grabbed a large piece of partially burnt wood from a funeral pyre and flung it towards the spot where I was standing.

But I was young, confused and desperate, and couldn't let go. "Why did you come to me in my dream, then?" I asked, on the verge of tears. "You spoke so sweetly and asked me to come and see you. That's why I came."

The madwoman's mood changed abruptly. She started cackling, in what felt like disturbingly unbalanced glee. "So, I went to talk to you in your dreams, is it? No, no! I went to chew up and eat your head! Go away, go now! Go, go, get out of my sight!"

While I was standing there and looking at her, it occurred to me that this madwoman had entranced me in some way. It felt as if the words of anger were superficial and didn't really count. She had got a hook in me in some way that counted, and she was pulling on that link, bringing me closer.

Her mood changed again. "Sit," she commanded. She pointed with a finger and made clear exactly where she wanted me to sit. The assuredness of the gesture seemed out of place in the setting of the cremation ground, and the company. It would have felt completely in place if an emperor had pointed a finger in that way in his own court.

There was no disobeying that command. I sat down.

"Tell me, why do you keep coming here and bothering me?" Her tone was almost caring. "You are not meant for the harsh life of spiritual discipline. I can see that you are deeply connected with the world, that you enjoy the pleasures it offers."

I offered no reply. A few minutes of silence later, the madwoman said, "I should ask you, are you hungry? Since you are here, would you like to eat something? What would you like?"

I wanted to test the limits of her power. People

said that if a sage or a godman was pleased with you, they would accede to any request, bring you whatever you wanted—I have seen that, with my own eyes, which is why the scented handkerchief from earlier this evening did not impress me—anyway, those are other stories.

Sitting there in front of the madwoman, I asked for a variety of confectionary that was not easy to make, and was probably not available locally. I also asked for a type of banana which was almost certainly available locally, but not common.

There were some half-burnt pieces of wood lying around. These were the ends of logs that had been used in pyres on the cremation ground. She picked some up and held them out to me.

"Here you are, the choicest sweets for you," she said.

Caught utterly unprepared, I gaped at the pieces. She saw my hesitation and burst into manic laughter. "Come on, take them and eat them," she said, "here are the best sweets for you."

A small part of me understood that her sanity was very much in question. Those were clearly left-over bits of funeral wood she was offering, wood that had been used to burn dead human bodies in this cremation ground. How could I possibly put them in my mouth? But the rest of me felt that I had travelled too far on this path to turn back. I had invested too much time, and too much energy to pass up any opportunity, no matter how strange, that came my way on this path of my choice. Perhaps I needed to accept that a certain amount of unpleasantness was inevitable on this path. Perhaps she would surprise me, and the pieces would turn into delicious sweets.

I took the half-burnt pieces from her and popped them in my mouth. The next moment, I was spitting out those awful, ashy, burnt bits of funeral-pyre kindling. Her high-pitched maniacal laughter surrounded me again.

The humiliation of that laugh brought unwanted tears to my eyes. This was a mistake, I thought, in anger and grief. The woman was genuinely unbalanced, there was nothing to be learned here. I had wasted my time. People talk like idiots, some idiot must have started the rumour that she had power, and other idiots passed it along.

The laughter stopped. "Did you enjoy your precious sweets, your bananas?" She was mocking me openly now. "You're just greedy, that's who you are. So, this is where you come to fulfill your greed for expensive things? To my cremation ground? Get out. Get out of this place at once."

I felt an upsurge of anger. No one had ever said anything this rude to my face before. I got up at once and left the place.

I know it sounds hard to believe, but she was back in my dreams very late that night, and not in the way you may think, given the experience of the day. I dreamt that she stood beside the bed and regarded me with a smile of tender care. "Don't be upset," she said gently, "come and see me today. No, there's no need to be angry now."'

Taranath barked a short, ironic laugh. 'Sometimes I still wonder if I knew that madwoman only in my dreams, or in real life too.

'Anyway, when I woke up the next day, all the bad feelings—the anger, the humiliation, the grief at a lapse in judgement and time lost—were gone so completely that it was as if I had never felt them. The thought crossed my mind that she had visited in a dream in order to bewitch me, but I was by then past master at ignoring those kinds of thoughts.

That afternoon found me back at the cremation ground. She looked peaceful and sounded friendly, "Ah, here you are, back again! I can see that you're very persistent."

"Why are you making me dance like this?" I asked her. "You insult me and send me away in the day, and call me to come and see you, at night. What could you possibly gain from driving me mad like this?"

She ignored my question. "Will you be able to do it?" she asked, in complete seriousness. "Do you have the courage to do it? Will you be able to do exactly as I say?"

"Yes, I have the courage," I said. "I'll do exactly as you say. Why don't you test me and see?"

Then she made the strangest proposition. "You must kill me tonight, strangle me with your hands," she told me. "Then you will have to sit on my dead body and meditate. I'll tell you how to do that correctly. You'll have to be prepared in advance, be sure to go and buy alcohol, fried flattened rice, and fried chickpeas from the market during the day. Occasionally, my dead mouth will open wide, and scream hideously. When that happens, just pour a swig of alcohol into my mouth, and follow it up with some flattened rice and chickpeas. You'll have to meditate all night sitting on my dead body. Be warned, you will be scared several times during the night. Those who will appear, in order to frighten you, they are not human. You must not be scared by them. The penalty for fear is very high. Not only will your efforts and meditation come to nothing, but you may also lose your life if you give in to the fear. Do you agree to do as I say?"

This was an unexpected test. I was stunned, hearing her words but recovered quickly. "I'll do everything else, but I can't kill a human being," I replied. "And why should you die for me?"

Predictably, she got angry. "Then why have you come here, you ungrateful wretch? Get away from here!" Ungrateful wretch was the sweetest thing she called me as her diatribe went on. She had a large vocabulary of rustic abuse, and no boundaries. But I had been toughened by the last few days in her company, and let her words wash over me without taking offence.

"Why are you getting so angry?" I asked, in a reasonable tone of voice, "Is killing someone such a simple thing, that you should get so angry with me? Am I not a gentleman?"

She twisted up her face as if there was a bad taste in her mouth. "A gentleman! Yes, indeed, you're a gentleman! Then why did you come to me, you useless, short-lived insect? Your life is so short that you're already a dead body! The path of tantra is no path for a gentleman. Go, wear your gentleman's clothes and work in an office, that's all you're good for! Leave, get out!"

"You're always getting angry," I replied, "think of all the problems with the police if I kill you. Who will save me when they pass a death-sentence and hang me?" I said these words calmly, but I had been genuinely rattled by her proposition. It was time to move on. This madwoman clearly had no gifts to give me. I felt a return of the hopeless sense of failure and wasted time that had set in the previous day.

Then I remembered all the pure Sanskrit rituals I'd heard her chant, and the small secrets of tantra she had occasionally revealed in her conversation. She could sound like a person of actual higher wisdom, when it suited her whims.

That was the day she arrived at a peace with me. When I went to the cremation ground in the evening, she called out to me of her own accord—"I don't remember anything when I get angry. The words just flow out of me. I abused you badly this morning, you mustn't mind that.

"It's a good thing that you refused the ritual I

asked of you. That kind of thing is a very lower-order accomplishment. You might have gained some small power from it, but that is all it would do."

I latched onto the word—power. "How do people gain power of this kind?"

"This earth has all kinds of beings which are invisible to the human eye. Once the body is emptied by death, what persists is something that we cannot see—we call it ghostkind. There are other beings too. Some of those have less intelligence than human beings, but much more strength. These beings are also invisible to humans. They are named in tantra, and Dakini and Shnakini are two such names. Unlike ghosts, these beings were never human. They are creatures native to the places humans go to when they die. Muslim spiritualists call them Djinns. There are good ones, and bad ones, and tantra can teach you how to call and control them. Once they are under your control, you can ask anything of them, and they have to obey. I mean that literally—they are compelled to do as you wish, they have no choice. But these are very dangerous beings, not at all to be called for entertainment, or to be trifled with. Even a moment of relaxed vigilance, or distraction, will be all that they will need to kill you."

Never having heard anything like this before, I listened to her with both astonishment and concentration. Indeed, words of this kind were appropriate only from the mouth of a madwoman. And not only a madwoman, but a madwoman in such a setting.

The cremation ground was rural, home to a large tamarind tree, a vast banyan, and a few red silk-cotton trees. There must have been a cremation a day or two ago because the burnt left-overs from the pyre and a water-pot used in rituals were lying by the edge of the water. The madwoman and I were the only people in sight. I knew that the area was deserted almost up to the nearest village, which was not close. An involuntary shiver of fear and goosebumps took over my body for a moment.

The madwoman was still talking when I came out of my reverie. All kinds of words poured out of her, such strange words that made little sense. "There is a kind of anti-god called Hakini in tantra. They are formidable beings. Much less intelligent than human beings but infinitely stronger, they have no concept of mercy. Their minds are like wild beasts. But they have such power! Once a tantrik is able to control them, once they are bound, they will do as they are told—and they have the strength to do almost anything. This is why a particular type of fearless tantrik chooses to call Hakini in meditation and ritual. Good for them, if it works out. But every step of that process is fraught with danger. Even a single misstep will kill the tantrik. This is why I have been trying to move you away from the path of tantra. There are too many perils and pitfalls. You get angry at me because you don't understand that I'm just trying to protect you."

Curiosity took over my tongue. "Then you know how to call and bind a Hakini, right? Tell me the truth!"

She made no reply, just sat there in silence. I realised that she had said all she was going to, for the time being. But I left that day convinced that the madwoman knew the means by which to reel in and harness the power of a fearsome Hakini.

Word of my comings and goings must have got out in the village, because I got several warnings from relative strangers the next day. I was warned against spending so much time at the cremation ground, and against associating so repeatedly and closely with the madwoman. "She has a lot of power," said one man, "she can destroy you, there will be nothing left. It is wisest not to mess with her."

"The people of our village have nothing to do with her," another man assured me. A third pointed out that I would know better if I was a local. But I was a stranger there. What would happen if she killed me, so far away from my home?

The warnings made no impact whatsoever. I was determined to learn anything she could teach me. I decided that she had probably already done her worst, what more could she possibly do? Besides, I did not have the strength to stay away from her.

I went to see the madwoman at the cremation ground every day, a few hours before dusk. One evening, I decided to approach her secretly, in a way that she would not be able to see me. I crept into the cremation ground, towards the banyan tree below which she normally sat, approaching it from the opposite side from the one she favoured.

She was missing. However, a girl who looked like she could be in her mid-teens was sitting at that spot, leaning comfortably back against the tree. If I was older I would have blamed my eyes for seeing wrong. But I was young and fit, and there was nothing whatsoever wrong with my eyes. Yes, there was a young woman in the cremation ground—where women of the village would never come unaccompanied—leaning casually against what I had come to think of as the madwoman's tree.

I had to assess this new situation. Did it pose some kind of threat I had not yet considered? Stepping forward slowly and cautiously I came out from behind the banyan tree and calmly asked the girl, "Where is she?"

The girl smiled, just as calm. "Who?"

"You know, the lady who stays here. Where is she?"

The girl dissolved into giggles. "Oh, that's funny! Why aren't you saying her name? Are you feeling too shy to say her name aloud?"

Light dawned on me. That laugh was familiar, but in an older person, so somewhat changed. Those words, too, I'd heard words like that before. So, the madwoman was present, but in a different form. It was the strangest feeling, to be faced with someone I knew and feared, who appeared to be speaking from within a quite pretty teenager.

The girl was still giggling. "Come," she said, through her laughter, "come closer, sit down, why are you staying so far away from me? Don't be shy, come here."

I suddenly felt afraid. Some instinctive sense was

telling me that there was something wrong here, that I should stay away from the girl. This was actually the madwoman, and I felt sure that she was trying to get me into trouble. I turned slowly away from her and started leaving the place.

I had barely taken a step or two away, turned my back on the girl for no more than a second or two, when a familiar voice greeted me from behind. I stopped in my tracks and turned slowly back towards the banyan tree. There she was, the madwoman, seated as usual at the base of the tree. The girl had disappeared, she was nowhere to be seen. My fear shot up a couple of notches. Enough for today, I thought. I need to get away from here as soon as possible.

"Come, sit," said the madwoman, in an entirely normal tone of voice.

"Why did you show yourself like a girl?" I wanted to know that before deciding what to do, "what were you planning?"

She deflected my question, "Oh look, the short-lived one is jabbering all kinds of rubbish!"

"No, I'm telling the truth." It took me courage to insist, but I couldn't just let this go. "Don't scare me now. Remember, I called you mother. You owe me that respect."

She considered something for a moment, and then said, "If you want the truth, here it is. You are not suited for this life of the spirit. You are too distracted by external appearance—that is not the way of tantra.

The power of tantra has nothing to do with dressing up and looking like a sage or godman, it is far deeper than that. This is not something you seem to understand.

"Anyway, you're very persistent, so I'll give you some small powers, ones that will help you earn a living in your own world. I need a dead body. Nothing to worry about on that front, there's quite a few dead bodies arriving soon to this cremation ground. Until then, we wait. There will be no power for you without a dead body. But once that happens, you will have to listen carefully, and do exactly as I say. Can you do that?"

My internal response was a kind of deep-seated urge to run away. I had never been a coward, but meditating on a dead body demanded a whole different category of courage. I had never imagined that I could be faced with a decision like this, in a situation in which such a thing could actually happen. But, here was also the possibility of real power, a thing I had dreamed of for as long as I could remember. I found myself saying, "Yes, I will do exactly as you say. My only condition is that I must not get into trouble with the police. Apart from that, anything you ask is fine with me."

A few days later, I went to the cremation ground shortly before dusk. She seemed filled with a suppressed excitement, but she was frequently strange without perceptible cause, so I ignored that. I got a glimpse into what she was thinking when she spoke.

"A dead body has been found. Come quietly."

There was a large peepul tree right at the edge of

the river, with part of its extensive roots feeding directly from the water. A few feet under the surface of the water, the body of a girl was trapped in those roots. She looked young—no more a child, but not yet a woman.

"Get that body," ordered the madwoman, "climb down the roots, get a grip on the body and lift it up. It'll be lighter in the water, you should be able to do this quite easily. Anchor it among the upper roots, close to the bank, so you can bring it to shore later. Mind, anchor it well. It must not float away in the current."

I obeyed her like an automaton. The body was wearing a garment that had become entangled in the roots of the tree, which is why it was trapped here. I climbed down, and it didn't feel like it took very much effort at all to untangle the garment and pull the body up, close to the surface. The madwoman was waiting close to where I came back up. "You'll have to sit on that body and meditate all night," she said, "you won't be scared, right? The moment you show fear, it'll all be over for you."

But I was not listening to her, I was looking at the body of the girl I had just brought close enough to the surface to see properly. It took me a few moments to register what I was seeing, and once my brain got the message, I let out a loud yelp of disbelief. Because the body which was clearly very dead, the one whose garments I had just untangled from the roots of the peepul tree, that body looked exactly like the teenage girl who had earlier been sitting under the banyan, the one who had turned out to be the madwoman. There was an absolute resemblance in every respect, face and body. This had to be the same person. There was no way it could be otherwise.

"Why are you shouting? Be quiet, no one should hear us." I started at her words, feeling that things had got all twisted up in my head. I felt a sudden, intense spike of cold fear. The people of the village had been right. This woman was indeed dangerous beyond belief.

But I had myself shut every route of return. I was here, at this moment, in this place. Once darkness fell, I would have to do exactly as she commanded.

This is how it proceeded. I completed the preliminary rituals as she directed, and sat on the corpse to meditate almost exactly as darkness fell. She had given me a largely meaningless chant, with orders to repeat it without change or pause until the beginning of light the next morning. Even with all the events that had occurred, and the fear I had felt, I did not believe that anything was going to happen as a result of this ritual. Even when she warned that I may well have fearful hallucinations—but no matter what happened, feeling fear or stopping the ritual would mean paying with my life—a stark warning, and a clear one—I did not quite believe her.

The hours rolled on. The cremation ground was absolutely quiet, I could hear no insects, not a single hoot of an owl. The darkness was also absolute, nothing was visible in any direction. There was no moon. I hadn't even noticed when the madwoman had left, or which way she had gone.

The silence was abruptly broken by the raucous call of a pack of jackals. It seemed to be coming from fairly close by, as if the pack was hiding in the thick bushes that grew wild in the cremation ground. I had heard a lot of wild jackals calling in the night at various times in my life. But I had never at the time been sitting on a corpse, in a place for the cremation of dead bodies, far distant from any comfort or help. The sound, and closeness of these jackals filled me with dread. Just then, another thing happened."'

Taranath paused, then went on, a little faster than before.

'Look, you can decide if you want to believe me or not. But do understand that I have no reason to lie to you. Our relationship is not one of transaction. I am Taranath the astrologer, I understand only money. You will not pay me at all. To me, that means that I have no cause to lie to you.

As soon as the jackals stopped calling, I heard a movement from the edge of the river. Women were walking out of the water and onto the shore. All kinds of women—young women, with their heads and faces covered to preserve modesty, middle-aged women who could be mothers, woman following woman, rising out of the river, with not a drop of water on their clothes or bodies. One, two, five, ten, twenty—

They came up and stood around, surrounding me. I concentrated fiercely on the chant, on keeping my concentration. Let things go ahead as they were fated, I would stay my course.

The fear abated in a little while. I opened my eyes properly and saw not women, but birds. There were lots of birds on the ground around me. I recognized them easily as korora birds, which I had seen before on the shores of the Birbhum river. When on the ground, they strut around in a self-important manner like little human beings.

I relaxed at once. Birds! Thank god! I was safe, after all!

I had barely finished the thought, when the laughter of many female voices exploded around me. It was a dry, cackling, unpleasant laugh, a kind of laughter that promised no good.

It seemed as if my blood froze to ice in my veins. I looked again, and there were no birds. There were only women. Right in front of me were the youngest of them. They had removed their head-coverings of modesty, and were standing there and looking straight at me.

I was in a sort of circular open space with the women in front of me. All around them, and me, were skeletons, human skeletons, standing arrayed rank after rank. I could see their gleaming bones through the pitch dark. There must have been a hundred skeletons surrounding me, maybe more. Many of them were old, missing fingers or other parts of limbs, discoloured and brittle by the long action of water or the sun. Some had skulls caved in, some had bones fractured and hanging at odd angles. Their bony heads were turned in different directions. They were static, utterly still. It looked almost like someone had installed them there, brought them all this way and lovingly set them up to give an overall effect, exactly so. The person who set them up might still be around, I thought incoherently. As soon as he lets them go, they will fall down in heaps of broken and fractured old bones.

But they were sentient somehow, those skeletons surrounding me. I felt that quite strongly. They were guards, not to protect me from any danger that may approach, but to prevent me from leaving the cremation ground alive. They were eager with anticipation. If I tried to leave, they would extend their hands of bone, place those broken fingers around my neck, and strangle me to death.

I was preparing myself to get up in one swift movement and start running, when I realised that another, quite different, woman had appeared from nowhere and was standing right in front of me. She was ethereally beautiful, and smiling, and she was blocking my way out. Who could this be? It didn't matter anymore. I had given up all illusion of control when I sat to meditate on a corpse. But before I could ask anything, she spoke. "I'm sixteen," she said. "I'm foremost among the Mahavidya, the supreme goddesses of wisdom. Don't you like me?"

I didn't know much about the supreme goddesses of wisdom, except fragments the madwoman had mentioned in passing. From that scattered information, I had gathered that it was very difficult to call them, and that the energy and time required was intense and long. But here was one of them. How was that possible?

"I am very fortunate that you have come," I said, in a properly respectful tone of voice. "I feel that the goal of my life has been fulfilled."

She said, "But why are you using these words? This is a very powerful prayer to a frightening being of supreme power. What is your reason for disturbing that power with your call?"

"My lady, I know nothing about the different kinds of prayer. I'm just doing as the madwoman told me to."

She thought this over. "I see," she said. "Well, then, it's time to stop saying those words. You have never seen the goddess who answers that prayer. Her aspect is terrifying, and not for human eyes to behold. It will scare you more than you can imagine."

I gathered together my courage and asked her the question that had been at the tip of my tongue since she appeared. "I have heard that it takes long, hard work to successfully call someone like you. How did you appear so easily to me?"

"Why? Do you doubt me?"

That face! It felt like I recognized that face for a fleeting moment, but the moment was gone almost as soon as it arrived. My mind was a mess, it felt unmoored, as if I was afloat in a dark, unknown place without any sense of direction or future. "I don't doubt you," I told her, "but I am filled with astonishment. I don't know anything about you, or what kind of being you may be.

Please forgive me if I insult or offend you, but I would really like an answer to my question."

The goddess said, "you don't know the Mahadamori, you don't know who I am. There's no point in you getting to know these things at this late stage. But you are asking why I am here, and that is a question I can answer. Have you heard of the Divaidya path in tantra? We use that path to descend to earth to answer the calls of you sinners. Your call was heard on the Divaidya path. That's why I came here, to see what was going on."

I did not quite understand what she said. The word sinner from such a powerful being had made me uncomfortable. "Am I very much a sinner, then?" I asked, in some fear.

She laughed like a girl. "I came at your call, to rescue human beings from the disaster you were about to bring down on them. Don't be afraid of me! Haven't I kicked you? Haven't I thrown wood from a dead pyre at you? Will I not test you, before I give you any real knowledge?"

What was she talking about? How could she say—

My confused mind stopped struggling because she was talking again. "But the supreme goddess of the Mahadamori is certainly not to be trifled with, consider this a warning. You're not very brave, you will not be able to deal with it if she does appear. Let that mantra be, stop chanting it."

"I will stop, if that is what you want me to do."

"Do you give me your word on that?"

"Yes."

At this point, my eyes happened to fall on the corpse on which I was sitting. In a horrorstruck flash, I remembered in full what had passed briefly through my mind earlier, the inkling of a familiarity with the goddess in front of me. A black fear descended before my eyes, starred with not a little astonishment. My whole body went utterly still. I think my heart may have stopped for a while. The being in front of me was ethereally beautiful and ornately dressed, yes, but beyond that surface gloss, she was absolutely identical to the dead body on which I was sitting, the one I had dragged out from between the watery roots of the peepul tree. The two had the same face, the same shade of skin colour, and they looked the same age.

The goddess had mockery in her smile, "What are you staring at?"

The hypnotic effect of clutching dread had passed. I was now suspicious, and I thought I knew what was actually going on. "Who are you really?" I asked her, no longer caring about letting my suspicion show, "are you the madwoman from the cremation ground?"

Everything changed the moment I spoke.

An enormous jeering laugh echoed from all around, ripping to shreds the silent darkness of deep night. Almost at the same time, the skeletons, which had been standing still and posed, started to move. They moved in fits and jerks, bones clacking and clanging and clashing against each other, making an incredible amount of disjointed sound. To my stunned eyes, it looked as if they were dancing to some beat that only they could hear.

Perhaps the unaccustomed movement was too much for the old bones, because the skeletons started falling apart as they danced. A hand fell off here, a leg there. I saw a spine fall away from one. Part of the skull of another detached and dropped to the ground. Another lost a rib, then one more, then two side-by-side lost all their ribs. But they kept moving, in their strange, jerky, disharmonious dance while the piles of fallen-off bones built up around them. In that fevered state it seemed to me that the bones continued to move even after they fell to the ground, heaps of bones sliding and clicking against each other in a vain effort to continue the dance that started while they were still attached to their skeletons. The heaps of bones grew as the dance continued, bone against bone, no intervening muscle or skin to muffle the raw, echoing, clattering sounds.

A part of the night sky crumpled and peeled away as if an invisible hand had ripped through paper. A figure of spine-tingling horror came through the gap, a monstrous female form of enormous power, an object of fear, the like of which I had never seen in my life. It started descending from the sky towards the earth. The jackals started howling again, louder and closer than before. A smell of many rotting organic things filled the air. Out of nowhere, the sky lit up in the throes of a fiery, blood-tinged sunset. Vultures appeared and started circling the sky, as if they were keeping an eye on prey on the ground. I couldn't keep track of light and dark, couldn't understand how any of this could be happening. My world narrowed to a pinprick filled with the sounds of clashing bone and howling jackals.

In that pinprick I heard the horrible sounds, and smelt the nauseating smells of putrefaction, but saw only one thing—that indescribably frightening figure in the sky, picking up speed as it moved closer and closer. It seemed to be heading straight in my direction, at speed, as if it was racing towards me. The eyes were ablaze with a blood light that was furiously angry and filled with unmeasurable malicious cruelty, even from a distance. Power exploded from her like a sun, an enraged supernova bent on the destruction of only one thing—me.

The corpse I was sitting on cried out suddenly. "Save me!" it pleaded, voice heavy with tears, "It is like this for me every single night! I am trapped because they murdered me, and I can't move on by myself—fifty-six years on this cremation ground! Who do I turn to? Who will hear me?"

All my resolution fell apart. I had reached my limit. This was impossible, I could not do this anymore. A very small part of my mind noted that the sky was starting to get lighter in the east, and I felt myself get off the girl's dead body, and start to run.

In reality, I had lost consciousness. When I came to, the madwoman was sitting in front of me, lost in thought and smiling slightly. She and I were the only beings under that banyan tree, and as far as I could see, on the cremation grounds.

She looked at me, still smiling. "Good, so now we know your limits," she said, without rancour. "You got off the body and ran."

I was still fuzzy and unfocused. "But I saw one of them," I replied, "The Goddesses of Knowledge you talked about, one of them came to me!"

The madwoman was looking very sane indeed. She suppressed a smile and said, "Yes, she appeared as a beautiful young woman, and you gave up on the chanting I had told you not to stop. You idiot. All of that was the controlling of minds that can be done by a Hakini. I warned you they were powerful. No Mahavidya would appear to you. And if by some remote chance one did, you wouldn't be able to recognize her even if she was sixteen and beautiful. Especially if she was sixteen and beautiful.

"You think it is so easy to call a goddess and have her answer? That this is all the effort it takes? No, what you saw was entirely illusion."

I felt both dismayed and suspicious at this dismissal of what I had experienced with such intensity through the night. "But she said so many things to me," I countered, "and even apart from her, I saw this terrifying witch-like monstrous woman."

The muddled confusion set in again. I could have sworn that the madwoman already knew all this, perhaps I had told her about it?

"You've had a very lucky escape," she said soberly. "That frightful monster you saw was an aspect of the supreme goddess. If she had reached, you would not have been able to withstand her power. Death would have been the only escape. But you didn't know that, so you tell me—why did you run?"

There was a short silence in which neither of us spoke. She broke it by starting to laugh loudly. "You worthless wretch! You think that you have seen the Supreme Goddess? These are eternal beings of infinite power that I dare not name too often—so I traffic in the lower-order Hakini—and you believe that they came to you and had conversations!

"You're so stupid that you didn't understand that I was weaving illusions for you. You've been sitting in front of me, beneath this banyan tree, the entire time since you entered the ground. What body? What chanting? And this morning, that you apparently sat till, which morning is that? It's just now getting to be dusk!"

What was she saying?

It was as if I awoke from a spell. It was indeed just going on dusk in the peaceful, quiet cremation ground. This woman was much more dangerous than I could have imagined.

I carefully cast my mind back, and saw it remembered everything clearly. Arriving at the ground around six o'clock at the beginning of a long midsummer evening, I had pulled the corpse out of the water. I remembered sitting to chant on the body, the skeletons dancing themselves into pieces, the beautiful goddess who asked me to stop my chant, the vultures circling overhead in a blood-red sky. How could this detailed memory be an illusion from start to finish?

I felt exhausted and numb, somehow distant from myself. "Why did you do this?" I asked her slowly. "Why go into all this trouble to deceive me, to make me believe so many lies?"

"You were so sure that you wanted to learn from me," she said. "I had to find out if you could do what you said you could. Now, I know for a fact that the path of tantra is not your path. Do not ever come this way again. Even if you do, you won't find me."

She sounded very final. But I had to ask one last question. "Tell me just one more thing," I said. "It's clear to me that you have power, more power than I imagined. Why, then, do you stay at the level of illusion? Why don't you try and access a higher level of tantra?"

For what felt like the first time, she actually looked at me. "I don't think that you are really capable of understanding that," she said. "The Mahadamori, the Mahavidya, these are incredibly difficult goals to attain. No one can do it in one lifetime, it takes several lifetimes of single-minded effort. This is what I did in my previous birth, and through this one. I haven't seen any sign of them yet. I have to keep trying, of course, but my efforts will very probably have to continue when I am born next.

"It's time for you to leave now, go on. There's no point discussing these things with you. I've granted you a few small powers, but I don't think you'll be able to keep them for too long. Go on then, go your way."

I came away. That was forty years ago. I never went

to the cremation ground again, out of fear, I think. I never saw the madwoman again.

I was young and very foolish, so I did not recognize it then, but now I think that the madwoman was no ordinary mortal. She presented the madness to shield herself from the curiosity of human eyes. About why she saw it fit to live in cremation grounds, near the freshly dead—how can we, as ordinary human beings, expect to find out or understand the reason for that?

Anyway, that's the story. The little power I had, was given by that madwoman. She was right though, it didn't last very long. I wasted it all away. Her assessment had been correct, I was far too attached to my greed for earthly things. Spiritual power flows away from you if you're like that. The only skill I still have left is knowing how to perceive the moon. Do you know how to perceive the moon? Let me show you. First, you cover your eyes with the fingers of both hands, then you use your thumbs to..."

***

I realised that Taranath would continue to talk as long as I was there, presenting him with an audience. It was late. I still had some important work to get done that day, work that was even more important than perceiving the moon.

You seem to want to know if I believed Taranath's long and complicated story? I will not answer this question.

The Second Story

THAT WAS THE first story that Taranath Tantrik told me. Perhaps, reader, you did not believe it. If you didn't believe that story, I don't particularly expect you to believe this one. But this second one is so exceedingly strange, that I could not keep from writing it down, even if it meets nothing but disbelief.

After all, how much do we actually know of the world around us? There are more things on this earth, Horatio—etcetera, etcetera. So do keep reading this story, but also keep in mind what the great poet said about the limits of our knowing.

But I should also add that this a story meant for those who feel, however subtly, that there may be other worlds beyond the veil of the obvious, beyond the things we can see or know in the physical, material dimensions. If your desire to understand the world stops at the veil of the obvious, you may choose not to read this very strange story.

Now for the story.

There was no work that day, so I'd gone to see a

football match. Turning towards home at dusk, I was somewhat depressed about the non-performance of my favourite team. Mohanbagan had lost. I reached Dharmatala and took an instant decision to detour, starting to walk towards nearby Motts Lane (can't remember the number), to the house of Taranath the astrologer.

Taranath greeted me cheerfully—'Here you are, come in, come in! I haven't seen you in a while! Where have you been?'

It took us some time to catch up with each other. I was getting ready to leave when it suddenly started to rain. This was not a drizzle, or even a slow steady rain which one can walk through, but a real downpour, the type of rain that envelopes everything and feels like it may never end. The kind of rain that may not last forever, but has no likelihood of ending soon. Taranath refused to let me leave while it was raining, so I sat back down. It felt like we were alone in the world, as we were in his living-room. Just him and me, and that rushing, roaring waterfall of rain.

A strange melancholy descends upon me when it rains like this. Let me explain. When it's not raining, it feels like all the people in the city may at any time crowd a path to my door. All the people of the city are not likely to visit me, of course, but dry skies mean that a possibility exists that they may. This possibility ceases to exist when it rains. No one is going to visit through the driving rain. When it rains, I am truly alone.

I felt that way in Taranath's house that evening, as if we were the only people in the city of Calcutta. Everyone else had simply disappeared into the rain. Darkness drew in, and the mood in the living room changed. Up to this point, our conversation had spanned a wide range of topics—why Mohanbagan had lost the game, the mysteriously low price of the current crop of mangoes, the tragic bus accident at Chowringhee that morning—but as an isolating dark fell through the torrential rain, the talk turned towards the confidential. We found ourselves in the sensitive conversational area of women and love.

Taranath may be a tantrik and a well-known astrologer interested in spiritual matters, but he had never been interested in celibacy. He had been open, if rather oblique, about his relationships with women, and I confess that I had a kind of prurient interest in drawing him to the subject. I was looking forward to a story packed with the kind of romantic detail that would satisfy my idle curiosity about his experiences. But I was completely unprepared for the story which followed. It was so strange, so utterly outlandish, that I was left with no idea what to think of it, or how to respond.

I would have leaned towards believing that he had made the story up, except that the expression on his face as he told it strongly suggested otherwise. However unbelievable, there must have been enough truth in it that it had caused him enormous pain in the past.

That pain still marked him, I could see it as he spoke. It reminded me of the times he would start to say something, and then cut himself off abruptly as if he could not finish the sentence. A shadow would cross his face at these times, and I would conclude that there was much more to Taranath's life and experiences than he had felt comfortable revealing to me. Perhaps it wasn't just me, perhaps he had not told those stories to anyone. Perhaps those were stories it was difficult to find the words to tell, or ones that should not be told at all, if only because the teller would surely be considered a liar.

I had started the conversation in a lighthearted way, 'My Lord Astrologer must have had a lot of experiences in this direction, what do you say?'

'Only one experience,' demurred Taranath, 'but one surpassing strange. It taught me what it is like to truly be in love. It feels like a long-ago dream now. Listen, if you must.'

I stopped him, 'I don't want to hear any tragic stories. She was your first love, she stole your heart, and then she died—was that what happened? Because I've heard that before, too many times!' Taranath laughed wryly. 'I'm very sure that you haven't heard this story too many times before. Listen to it, and tell me if you don't believe it. If I had the ability to make up stories like this, I would have become a writer. No one but one or two close friends have heard this story before.'

At this moment, Taranath's eldest daughter entered the room from the inner part of the house, with two cups of steaming tea and hot savouries. Chari was about fourteen, fair like her father, and pretty. She was not happy with me, 'Uncle, why didn't you bring me a picture of the lace?' She asked. I had promised Chari pictures of a particular pattern of lace from a shop in Dharmatala. She wanted to use it to make a pattern of her own.

'Dharmatala was too crowded after football for me to get to the shop.' I said, 'I promise I'll get it for you tomorrow.'

Chari didn't look like she was finished talking, and Taranath got impatient. 'Go now,' he told her, 'get me two of the paans I like, go.'

She left without argument, and he relaxed. 'These stories, I can't tell them with the children hanging around. Now drink your tea, and eat everything on your plate while it's still warm, no, no you can't set any of it aside. Young man, this is your time to enjoy good food! Wash your hands in the rain. Right, now—'

***

I finished my tea and settled down to listen.

Taranath began his story.

'I told you about the madwoman in the Birbhum cremation ground. I left and came away immediately after that event I told you about. But I had developed a deep respect for teachings of tantra. After all, I could not refuse to believe the power I had seen with my own eyes! I understood that the madwoman had held me with magic that she could wield because of her knowledge of the lower orders of tantra. But she had also mentioned other, higher orders of tantra, that gave the practitioner unimaginable power. Now my curiosity was truly awakened about the potential of this kind of spiritual practice. Once more, I started looking for a teacher.

I didn't find one. I did find out though that true teachers of tantra were rare and difficult to find.

A lot of travelling later, I had learned two valuable lessons. First, that there was a large number of the type of spiritualist who lights incense and mumbles incantations as a substitute for being a practitioner of actual power. These fake spiritualists were always principally interested in business. Spirituality was a commodity to them, to be bought and sold at a price. Many of them had invested in detailed and complex strategies to fool their followers into believing that they were in the presence of true power. The second thing I learned was that most regular people are very, very stupid. It is extremely easy to fool them, especially in matters of belief and devotion.

But never mind regular people. I saw lots of business-spiritualists, even more karma insurance salesman, and more than a few self-proclaimed practitioners selling amulets and snake-oil. I even met some true ascetics, who wander without belongings and beg to survive. What I did not see even one of was a sadhu, a being of elevation, a true practitioner of tantra. I was losing hope of ever meeting a true teacher. But not yet ready to give up altogether, I continued to search.

One day, I happened to come upon a small temple in the middle of a Sal forest on the banks of the Barakar river. There was a tiny village—just a few houses—some distance beyond the edge of the forest. But dusk was falling rapidly on a chilly winter evening, so I took shelter in the temple. Having gathered enough dry twigs and branches to light a fire, I was preparing to settle in for the night, when another person, a man, entered the temple. He was somewhere between middle-aged and elderly, tall, straight, big at the shoulders, and dark-complexioned. He carried a small bundle of personal possessions under one arm.

I instantly recognized him as different in some undefined way. Before my brain could fully process this idea, I stumbled to fall prostrate on the ground in front of him, in the manner of true devotees everywhere.

He spoke sweetly, "I can see your faith runs deep! What are you looking for, here? I see that you have left home in anger!"

"Not anger, my sage, it was indifference to the material world—," I started to say in tones of subdued protest, but the man cut me off with a laugh. "You can't just say—I'm going to be a sage—and become a sage. Your desires are entirely of the material world. Go, be a householder!"

The madwoman had told me the same thing. But I was stubborn, and I stayed.

A short distance from the temple, there was a devil's tree, which we call chatim. He had a seat under that tree. It was a proper panchamundi asana, with a level space for one person to sit cross-legged in the centre, and five severed human heads at five corners. He would sit on it and meditate all night. I would watch him in awe, from a distance. This was it, I decided. He was the real thing, an advanced practitioner of tantra. I was not going to leave this man, this opportunity to learn. No matter what happened, I would stay. I became his only full-time follower, gathering all the wood for his fire-rituals every day. I would walk three miles to the village of Kusumbani to buy his basic provisions.

On these visits beyond the forest, I learned that most people in the surrounding villages regarded him as a powerful tantrik. He had done many strange things that could not be explained with logic, and his skills were not understood, but spoken of with care. I also got the kind of warnings I recognized from the villages around the madwoman. He's a powerful man, they told me. There's no trusting those who have this kind of spiritual power, they said. Who knows what a person of power is actually capable of, if they turn their minds towards things that are not good? The general verdict was that I should be careful and not get involved too deep. Trouble was clearly forecast if I insisted on continuing my current course.

They were right.

One night I woke suddenly from a deep sleep. It was

a day past the full moon, and the glowing moonlight lay bright on the ground. I got up and moved to my usual spot to watch the sage on his terrible seat. To my surprise, there seemed to be someone with him. He was sitting in his usual place, and talking to someone who was hidden from me by the trees. My curiosity spiked instantly. Who could he be talking to, so late at night, in this desolate forest by the river?

I inched forward carefully until the other person was partly in view. What I saw left me somewhat shocked, and utterly confused. He was talking to a woman. She was standing in front of him, just beyond the seat. Not only was she a woman, in itself a surprising thing at that time and place, she seemed young, and, as far as I was able to see in the play of light and shade through the leaves, very beautiful.

How was this possible? How could a young woman have come here, to this forest so far from human habitation, at this very late hour? Where could she have come from? I would have to move further forward to see her clearly, but they would have become aware of my presence if I did that. The idea that those two figures would catch me eavesdropping on their private conversation gave me a sudden shiver of fear. Enough for tonight. Still very carefully, I turned back towards the temple and went to bed.

I didn't sleep the next night. I waited until it was very late, then as quiet as a shadow, I tiptoed to watch from behind the shelter of the trees. She was there, talking to him, exactly like the night before. I watched them talk all night. As the sky lightened towards dawn, I became afraid of being seen and turned back to the temple.

The next night was exactly the same.

The night after that I noticed something about his visitor, the woman. It seemed to me that she was dressed in quite a strange way. I couldn't identify the garments she was wearing, or where they may be from. She wasn't in a single cloth draped like a sari, or a top-and-bottom set like a ghagra, or a stitched sheath like a kimono, or a gown. I could not recognize the garment, but whatever it was, I had to admit that it suited her beautifully.

Sometime during my watch that night the thought crept into my head that she knew I was there, hidden behind the trees, staring at her. Not only was she aware of me at that moment, she had known of my voyeurism every night, from the first time I had taken position behind the tree on that first night. I have no idea what caused this idea to take shape in my mind, but as soon as it did I started to feel very uncomfortable, and a little scared. I moved away immediately. It's not your business, just let it be, I counselled myself. What would be the point of getting entangled in whatever complicated situation this certainly was?

The self-applied caution did not last very long. I lay awake the next night, tossing and turning, unable to sleep. Eventually, almost from a lack of something to do, I found myself at the familiar place behind the trees looking at the woman. I noticed another thing that night. When she was there, a faint and lovely fragrance seemed to suffuse the area. I had smelt it every night I watched her, but had upto that moment failed to connect it to her presence. The forest had all kinds of scented wildflowers, some opened at night. I had thought I was smelling a flower that bloomed near the temple. That night however, I felt certain that the fragrance was, and had always been somehow connected to her person, her presence in the forest.

This state of affairs continued for the next ten or twelve nights. I watched them talking through the night, every night, carrying in my head the niggling suspicion that the woman with the intoxicating fragrance knew I was there. It was not an altogether pleasant thought. But once the night got dark, I could not keep away from my hiding place behind the trees.

Then, a summons came for the tantrik. A wealthy zamindar somewhere near the town of Barakar, or Koderma, was having trouble with bad spirits on his property. He had sent a request to the tantrik to come and use his powers and rituals to restore peace to the property. The request came on two consecutive days, via two different messengers, and was turned back both times. It was clear that the tantrik did not want to travel at all.

On the third day, the zamindar's younger brother arrived in a palanquin, carrying the request himself. He pleaded his family's need to the tantrik, and after much effort, succeeded in persuading him to travel to resolve the supernatural problem.

I was convinced that I knew why the tantrik had been so reluctant to travel for work. It was simple, really. He had not wanted to lose even a single night in the company of the beautiful woman with the intoxicating fragrance. I understood that completely. What I did not understand was the mystery of where she came from. There was no habitation within walking distance that could be home for someone like her. It was evident to me that she was not local. The locals were a dark-skinned people, the original inhabitants of the forested area. I had looked at her long enough to see that she was fair, and beautiful in a way that indicated high birth. Her look, the refined gestures, the rich fabric from which those unknown clothes were made, all indicated wealth. So, who was she, and where was she from?

A mischievous idea surfaced in my head. The tantrik had left during the day, with the zamindar's brother. Perhaps he had not had the opportunity to inform the woman that he would be gone—in which case there was chance that she would come again tonight. I resolved to find out more about her if she did. In my defence, I was a young man, harebrained and impatient. What you call romance was whirling through my mind, blanking out any good sense. Can you blame me for that?

That night, I waited until it was late. Some time before their usual meeting time, I went and seated myself on the tantrik's dreadful seat with the five dried and shrunken human heads, and waited. I was overwhelmed by a sense of romantic mystery. Would she come? Would I finally get to meet her?

The night was silent and utterly still. Slowly, the curiosity that overwhelmed me became underlaid with a little lurking fear. I had never done anything like this before. What if I got into some kind of serious trouble?'

I was young then, so young. I knew nothing, had no capability to look ahead. If I had even an inkling of the scale of trouble I was bringing into my life, do you think there would have been the slightest chance of my sitting on that five-headed seat? I have thought later that it was the invisible writing on my wall. Only fate could have decreed such consequences to an action, consequences that reach through all the intervening years and continue to impact my life. A temporary lapse of reason one ill-fated night, and a lifetime of gritty residue at the bottom of life's cup from that moment.

But never mind that, let's get back to the story.

'So there I was, sitting on the tantrik's seat under the chatim tree. The moon floated up from behind the trees to my right, and the night got later and quieter. The seat was very close to the rocky bank of the Barakar river which flowed to my left. Both sides of the river were strewn with boulders and rocks, on which the moonlight shone bright. There were no trees to cast a shadow and hide anyone approaching the seat on that side. On my other side, there was a grass meadow—not large, but big enough that anyone approaching from that direction would find no concealment as they walked towards the seat. The trees of the forest started where the clearing ended. I kept a sharp watch on all sides.

Suddenly, there she was, in front of me. It was very abrupt. One moment I was looking at an empty moonlit vista, the next instant she was there, just beyond the seat. It was literally impossible for her to be there. I would have seen her as she negotiated the boulders and rocks on the banks of the river, and I would have most definitely seen her if she walked out of the forest and towards me. There were no other possible approaches. I know this for sure because I had plotted all the possible paths over days. How could she be there, when even half a second ago, there was empty space all around?

Even through my whirling thoughts, I smelt that distinctive fragrance. As soon as I registered the scent, it felt like my whole body went numb. Then I stopped thinking, because my mind had gone blank. A few seconds after this I felt my vision dim in the way it does when you slide towards unconsciousness. I have no idea what happened after that.

I returned to myself at dawn and realised that I had been lying unconscious in that dreadful five-headed seat all night, exposed to the elements. My whole body was aching, my voice heavy in a way that signalled a developing block in the sinus. I got up to slowly return to the temple, and lay down once again. Illness was close, definitely a bad cold, perhaps even chills and a fever.

I ate nothing and stayed in bed that day. All I did was constantly turn over in my head the incident with the woman. It was impossible, she couldn't possibly have got to the seat through the areas I was watching like a hawk. And how incredibly beautiful she was! Even in the few seconds I was conscious, I had been struck by her utter loveliness. And then, about losing consciousness. Why had I fallen unconscious? That made no sense at all! None of it made any sense, but I could not resist picking it apart to examine the details for meaning. I did not understand any of it even after an entire day of worrying at the incident of the previous night from every angle.

The tantrik returned that evening. He had evidently thought of me, because he brought gifts—sweets, savouries, and a nice length of sturdy fabric—marks of appreciation he had received from his grateful hosts. They had expressed their gratitude through a warm, high-quality set of clothes for him, and these gifts for me.

"Why are you in bed?" he asked, "get up and put these things away."

I somehow got up and took the bundle of gifts. The struggle to move must have been obvious, because he looked a little concerned, "What's happened to you? Are you not well?" I did not respond.

He went off to have a bath. When he returned, all he wanted to talk about was his experiences at the zamindari house, how they live, how well they treated him. To me he said, "Will you tell me what happened to you? Why are you so depressed? Are you missing home? I keep telling you, you're a young man, and this is not a path for young men. You can't walk this path just because you decide that you must. This is a very difficult path!"

I fell seriously ill that night with a high fever. Time passed, but I had no way to tell how much time. I lost consciousness for long periods. But whenever I opened my eyes, there was the tantrik, hovering, worried. His care was the only thing that anchored me to this world, and he pulled me through the illness and out at the other end. I got slowly better.

One afternoon when I was feeling well again, and had sat down at my customary meditation-spot, the tantrik asked me, "You may be young and thoughtless, but do you know how much trouble you could have got into? You would not have survived this illness, it took a lot of effort to keep you with us. Why did you go and sit on my seat that night?"

I was shocked. I had certainly not told him about my transgression, and the events that followed. How had he come to know about it? That strange woman must have met the tantrik while I was sick. She must have told him.

He regarded my silence, then guessed the cause correctly. "You're wondering how I got to know of what you did? You have to understand that you—not just you, but the people belonging to the material world—don't know very much, most realities of this universe are hidden from you. And you—all of you—understand even less than you know. Sometimes, I look at you and feel pity at how little you understand."

I was embarrassed, and not a little worried. But I had to find out, even if only for my own satisfaction. "How did you know?" I asked. He laughed briefly. "You told me. All those days in the depths of fever, while I tried my best to ensure that you lived—and almost failed—you talked right through them and told me everything. Anyway, you survived this time. Never try to do something that stupid again."

If I had been embarrassed before, that was nothing compared to how I felt now. So I had told him everything? I silently swore to myself that this chapter of my life was done, that I would be on my way in a day or two, or as soon as I was able to travel.

But fate decreed otherwise. A scorpion bit the tantrik the next evening, and he was in excruciating pain. I ran five miles to Mihijam to get the nearest doctor. For three days and nights I cared for him as he had for me. On the fourth day, he had recovered enough that it was clear the danger had passed.

About ten days after that, I told him, "Sadhuji, I want to go away from here, today."

He looked taken aback, "You want to go? Where?"

I was determined to tell the truth as I saw it. "What's the point of staying? It's not like I'm learning anything here, I'm just taking up a share of donations from devotees. They're your devotees, what they give should be yours. I don't want to stay and continue to eat from your donations."

He didn't say anything.

A little before dusk, he called me to his side. "I had thought that I would protect you from this dangerous path. But I don't want you to be unhappy when you leave. You have done so much for me, especially in these last few days, that I would be upset if you left me feeling sad and disappointed. I want to give you something, a parting gift. But tell me, do you think of yourself as courageous?"

This was firm ground. "Yes," I said at once. "Before this, I was in Birbhum. I meditated to learn tantra at a cremation ground there." Then, I told him the full story of my experience with the madwoman. This was the first time a reason had come up to speak of it to him. He was astonished. "You know her? She's a very powerful, dangerous woman. That you escaped her with no damage can only be put down to good karma, perhaps from a previous birth. People call her Matu the Madwoman, but her actual name is Matangini. She knows everything there is to know about the lower rungs of tantra, of the black magic kind. Even we keep our distance from her, fear her too, do you know why? Because she is unstable, a complete wildcard, no one knows in which way she will choose to wield her power in any situation. So, like you keep away from a poisonous snake, or a rabid dog, we avoid her company and her wrath. But her power, and skill at using it, is extraordinary! She has a rather strange history, I'll tell you about it some other time. How long were you around her?"

"Almost two months."

The tantrik stayed quiet for a little while. "You spent time with her, so some small advancement along the path may be due to you," he said thoughtfully. "Yes, I will teach you. But you are young, and I know how you think. Tell me truthfully now, why did you go and sit on my seat that night?" The truth was that I had sat on his seat entirely in the hopes of meeting that beautiful, mysterious, night-travelling woman. Staying quiet seemed preferable to confirming his evident suspicions, so I stayed quiet. I couldn't possibly reveal myself like that to someone who I thought of as an elder and teacher.

That day, he told me a strange and secret thing. "Before we move any further, there's something you do need to know. The woman you met that day, under my chatim tree? She's not really a woman. She's not even a human being with blood and flesh and bones like you or me." An involuntary shiver passed through me at his words. What did that mean, that she was not human? If not a human with a physical body, then what was she, that exquisite woman? Was she a ghost? A witch?

He sighed. "I would not tell you any of this," he said, "except that you survived Matu the Madwoman, and that changes how I see you. All right then, let me go on. I learned the way of tantra from a great sadhu called Kalikananda Brahmachari. His ashram was located in Hooghly district, at a village called Jejur. That is where his students and devotees gathered. He was very powerful in two strains of tantra, Kularnob and Mahadamor. You should know that it is very rare for one individual to hold equal mastery over two such difficult spiritual domains." The tantrik talked for a while, telling me about the various paths of tantra and what they did. Among other things, I learned that Mahadamor is itself divided into several strains, some in the lower tantra, and some in the higher. One of lower strains is called Bhutdamor.

Bhutdamor! My ears picked up at once. I understood bhut as ghost, which is how the word is commonly used. What a magnificent skill that would be to possess! I was young then, you see, maybe as young as you are now. These were the types of things that interested me about the unknown. I must have shown my enthusiasm on my face, because the tantrik, who was now my teacher, read my expression correctly. He tried very hard to dissuade me. But the invisible writing of fate cannot be erased, and my future was already written—'

'Why did your teacher try to turn you away from that path?' I interrupted him.

'He said it was the path of temptation, of danger. The incantations of Bhutdamor call on various kinds of disembodied supernatural beings. These are beings of a great deal of power, like gods and goddesses, but not exactly. They are more the opposite of how the divine is supposed to be. We propitiate them by calling them gods and goddesses though some of these are outright demons. They are called jogini in the language of tantra. The identity of each jogini is embedded in the incantations and rituals you use to call it. If you are successful in your devotion to that call, the powerful supernatural being of your choice will be yours, to do with as you wish.

Each of them are different, and can be in different relationships with the caller. The jogini Kankini Devi, for example, always comes to the devotee as a mother-figure. Kanakbati Devi will only come as a daughter. The others are more flexible, they will come to you in the form you call for them. Among these beings, some are better to humans, and some are worse, but all of them are amoral. There is no morality, no conception of values in their world, no judgement, no beliefs or faith. They have no limits, and are tied by no rules.

The first incantation of Bhutdamor begins the propitiation of the jogini to which the call goes out. It says that if the devotee is able to complete the many complex incantations and rituals successfully, she or he will gain all of the eight superior supernatural powers. This knowledge is secret, and profoundly difficult to acquire.

"You saw the woman," the tantrik said, "she's the kind of powerful, amoral being the Bhutdamor incantations call. If you feel that you have the courage to follow that path, I am willing to teach you the way. But do take my warning seriously, that path is fraught with peril, sometimes when you least expect it. I would not recommend that you get on that path."

It was too late for the warning, he had said too much already. I had heard enough to be buzzing with the desire to find out more. His words of warning passed over without leaving the slightest mark.

My teacher read my face correctly, and tried to minimize the possible damage. "If you insist on this path," he said, "let me teach you the ways to call Kanakbati Devi. She will come as a daughter, you will cherish her—"

He stopped, even though I hadn't said a word. "Then, Kankini Devi? Would you learn how to call her?"

How annoying of the moralistic old man! I thought. Why is he dragging his heels so much? Why does he have such a problem teaching me how to call the other joginis, the ones who have forms other than mother and daughter?

The tantrik gave up. "Fine," he said. "I'll teach you the ways to call Madhusundari Devi. You can call her as a daughter, sister, or lover. But please listen to me and never call her as a lover. Let me tell you why. If you call her as a lover, she will think of you as a lover, a suitor, too. But these powerful beings are nothing like ordinary women. There is no way to predict, or even understand what they are capable of doing, or may do. I told you before, they have no ethics, boundaries, or limits. She could make you the happiest man in the world, or you could end up a stark raving lunatic. There's no telling which it will be. Are you sure that you can deal with that?"

In spite of his clear misgivings, he taught me the incantations and rituals to propitiate and call Madhusundari Devi. Then he told me, gently and with affection, that I would have to leave. "I can no longer keep you here," he said, "because two followers of tantra should not be meditating at the same place."

That was fine with me. I didn't want to stay either. Truth to tell, I had been afraid that he would end up behaving like Matu the Madwoman, use hypnotism to show me all kinds of terrifying otherworldly things. I doubted that I would survive another showing of those things.'

'Why would you think that?' I interrupted Taranath. 'You saw the woman with your own eyes. He wasn't around to hypnotize you when she came that night.'

He acknowledged me with a nod, then went on.

'It turned out that I had quite a bad case of typhoid. Haven't I said that before? No? The timing of the illness made me wonder if I was already hallucinating that night I sat on the tantrik's seat. Maybe the woman did not come to me, maybe it was just a fever dream. I did consider this seriously once the typhoid had passed.

Once I was wholly recovered, I walked five or six miles along the river and found another desolate spot.

There was no convenient temple to sleep in, so I stayed at the charitable dormitory in the nearby village. I would eat only whatever food the village-folk gave in alms, and each evening I would walk to my chosen spot at the riverbank and spend most of the night meditating and reciting the incantations the tantrik had taught me.

One, two, three months passed this way. No beautiful woman appeared to me, nothing whatsoever happened. I started to doubt the power of the incantation the tantrik had given. But I did not stop, because he had told me that no effect would come of the practice before a minimum period of six months. I would have to conduct a fire-ritual and some other practices at the end of the six months for it to be effective.

When the six months were done, I followed all the instructions he had detailed to me. I lit a small fire on the bank of the river, and cooked rice on it. I caught a type of perch fish from the river, and roasted that over the open fire. A particular type of banana leaf was required to serve the offerings in this ritual. I had earlier found a clump of that banana tree in the forest and harvested some leaves. Arranging the offerings of boiled rice and charred fish on one of these leaves, I lit the ritualistic fire with fig-wood, on sand. All this time, I had to be sure that the incantations were correct for the part of the ritual that went with each gesture. It was detailed and complicated.

One of the things it needed was a particular type of jasmine that did not grow anywhere in the area. I had managed to get a few of these flowers from a village some distance away, and made a garland. This I arranged on another banana leaf, with sandalwood paste and some smaller required items. Then I sat in meditation with the offerings arranged in the prescribed order in front of me. It took the whole night to complete the incantations and rituals that the tantrik had taught me for the six-month point on this path—'

'Did you see anything?' I asked. Taranath continued as though I had not spoken.

'—so many intricate arrangements! I had spent almost all my money buying the clarified butter, high-quality sandalwood, and particular sweets that this ritual required. By the time dawn lightened the sky, it was clear that all this time, preparation and expense had come to nothing. I was angry, and very frustrated, and fighting inside with the strong suspicion that I had been tricked again. Reaching out with this anger I swept up all the myriad hard-to-get items of the ritual in both hands, and tossed them into the river.

I was convinced that the man I thought of as a tantrik had lied to me about everything. Not only had he made up all the complicated rituals and incantations that were supposed to be a parting gift, he was himself a fake, a hollow actor with no spiritual knowledge or power. In essence, he was just like the madwoman in Birbhum, only subtler and more deceptive. I had wasted so many months of my life on this fakery, this absolute sham. There was no truth in the words—his words, or the pretend-words he had made up in the incantations. Perhaps he knows a little hypnotism, and uses that to fool the local villagers into giving him what he needs to keep living in their temple.

It was easy to think these uncharitable thoughts, but giving up on the daily rituals was harder. They had become habits, integrated into my life. Each evening found me at my customary place by the Barakar river, sitting in meditation for long hours, still and quiet. Another four or five months went by in this way.

I was seated under my favourite tree one late dusk, when I became aware of the faint smell of musk in the air. Listen carefully, now. I'm not lying, or even exaggerating in the slightest. I'm just telling you things as they happened one after another, so listen closely.

Since I was deep in meditation, it took a few seconds for the smell of musk to register on my consciousness. It was with a smile that my mind turned towards the smell. What a wonderful fragrance, I thought, nature is truly magnificent in her bounty! Immediately after this my senses sharpened because it felt as if someone was standing behind me, on the other side of the trunk of the tree. It is true that I could not see the person, but that made me no less sure of their presence. Sometimes instinct serves better than eyes. My entire being was suddenly, completely awake and alert.

The air went still. Then, I felt as if my body was on fire, burning embers scorching my insides and exploding outward. The excruciating pain was growing. Was I about to faint again? Just at that moment, the pain disappeared, and there was a woman standing in front of me. I was absolutely certain that she had not been anywhere near that spot even a heartbeat ago. The suddenness echoed exactly that night when I occupied the tantrik's seat. But this time I knew that she had come for me. This time, I would not slide into unconsciousness. I looked at her. She seemed to be frowning in disapproval—'

***

'Are you sure you saw this woman yourself, with your own eyes?' The question slipped out of my mouth before I could stop it. Taranath heard my disbelief, and his tone became agitated and defensive—'Did I see her with my own eyes? Of course I saw her with my own eyes! There she was, large as life, standing in front of me! Look, you can believe me or not, that's up to you. But you can't say that I'm lying to you, because I'm not.'

'What did she look like?' I asked, hoping to appease him somewhat.

'If I said she was beautiful, that would be less than a proper description. She was exactly as the incantation to call her says, a loveliness beyond words, beyond compare, beyond this world. I realised that the incantations of power I had been pronouncing for months were not simply words made up to call this being, they were descriptions of her power and beauty.'

'Did you talk to her?' I was hanging on to his words.

'Talk to her?' he scoffed. 'I was just barely hanging onto consciousness, and you want to know if I talked to her! This was not a normal woman, you understand? Not from any point of view was she ordinary. Her power radiated from her like the sun. And those eyes! The incantation to call her mentions her eyes, I had thought those were just words to propitiate the goddess and compel her to respond to the call. My god, you should have seen those eyes—worlds could be conquered and burn in the fiery steel of those exquisite eyes.'

I became impatient. 'Never mind the long descriptions! What happened? What did you talk with her about?'

He became circumspect. 'What we talked about is private, between her and me. Such things are not for others to know.'

***

'What happened is that Madhusundari Devi started to visit me every night. In that desolate place by the river, I had called her as a lover. But you must have guessed that already. After all, who could possibly be dull enough to listen to overcautious warnings from an old tantrik?

It was a mild winter. The waters of the Barakar river were gentle, and low in the bed. The lilies in the shallow water near the banks had become dry and yellow, revealing rock-minerals in the sand that sparkled in the light of the moon. The forests on both sides of the river were shedding leaves into the breeze. The skies were clear and blue in the day, and the moon shone in a cloudless sky at night. From that time on, for three months, she visited me every night. I felt completely alive in those three months, never before, or since, have I felt like that. It's painful to talk about feeling like that now.

You cannot imagine the pain of it, the grief of loss over a self capable of that kind of joy. I reached a pinnacle of happiness and stayed there for three whole months. She was a goddess indeed. No ordinary human woman would be able to grant such experiences of love, such deep, perfect friendship. Being with her was heavenly, not of this earth. I can't explain it to you. What words would I use? And you would disbelieve me anyway. You'd call me a liar, or say I'm mad. Perhaps you're thinking those things right now, as I gabble on. It's not just you, even my wife does not believe me. She says the tantrik had used his black magic skills to shut my brains down.

That kind of happiness is intoxicating, like being drunk on very strong wine. But being drunk on strong wine also creates an ennui of its own. I would be listless all day, nothing in this real world held my interest. The daylight hours would go in longing for the evening. When would dusk darken to twilight under the trees, in the forest by the river? When would she appear, my beautiful actress, perfect heroine to my new-found role as hero? The nights would pass like a dream, time slipping through my fingers like dry sand, each night deeply intoxicated and glittering with joy. My consciousness would expand outwards, grow unfettered, till the sky, the planets, the gods and goddesses were all part of my being, each night, under the stars by the river.

Then, something happened.

A young woman who lived in the nearby village used to come to the river to get water. Since she came every day, I saw her quite regularly. She was quite attractive, in the way the local women often were. I had felt her observing me a few times, so I watched her too. That day, she had filled her pot at the river and turned homeward, when she addressed me in the local dialect, "I have had babies, but they all died. Do you have an amulet to keep them alive?" She looked and sounded so sad that I immediately wanted to help her if I could. I didn't claim to have any protection for her unborn children, but we talked for a short while. Then she went on her way.

That day, I saw another aspect of Madhusundari Devi. How she grimaced with her whole being, and focused a terrible anger on me. You cannot imagine that expression, how her face twisted with rage. I saw a furious, vengeful goddess that day, Chandika turning into the dreadful destructive aspect of the goddess Kali in front of me. It was terrifying.

It started with a putrid smell suddenly filling the forest, as if a massive carcass was rotting nearby. Then she appeared. One look at her, and it was clear that the being in front of me was enormously powerful like a god or a goddess, but it was not a being of divinity. It was something else. It was a thing with no ethics, no borders, capable of anything that it wanted to do. The hands I had seen making delicate garlands with night-blooming wildflowers, on a whimsy, were also accustomed to destroy whatever displeased it, on whimsy.

It was then that I truly understood that my lover, who had turned my life into a heaven of bliss, not only was she certainly not a woman, she was also nothing like a human being. No matter how angry a human woman gets with you, she will always remain an angry human woman. She will never turn into an incandescent, raging goddess of destruction, or a powerful flesh-eating demon.

I was frozen with fear. The demoness Madhusundari sensed my fear. "Why are you afraid?" she asked.

I returned to myself. "What fear?" I asked hurriedly. "Why are you angry?"

The demoness' rattling, gravelly, hollow laughter filled the forest. This time, my spine felt like a freezing hand had reached into my back and gripped it. "Do you want to know everything?" The menacing figure ground out, threateningly, "if, in the dark of night, some anonymous local woman's dead body drifts down the river in front of you, will you know it? You may not know it, but if two dead bodies drift down the river, intertwined, the other locals will definitely recognize them in the morning."

I realised to my horror that it would be a matter

of a moment for the demoness to do as it threatened, that it was not a being that could be reasoned with. I sank down on my knees and put my hands together in supplication. "Goddess, I love you, and only you! I beg you, please do not frighten me like this! I am your lover, you can kill me if you wish, but have mercy on that innocent village woman, please have mercy!"

It took most of the night, and reserves of energy I didn't know I had, but I begged and pleaded and promised, and propitiated her rage. Once her anger had faded, there she was, back again in the form of the beautiful woman to whom I had given my heart. It was as if the enraged demoness had never existed.

"Do you want to see me like that woman?" she asked sweetly. "I can be just like her." Before I could make any reply, the village woman I had talked to earlier was standing in front of me. No, not her, exactly, but a version of her that was more beautiful, more desirable.

I panicked even through my exhaustion. "No, no, I don't want her," I cried, "I want you, the way you are with me, goddess!"

From that time on, I felt that I had entered an arena with a particularly venomous, particularly unpredictable snake. This is why the old tantrik had warned me away from the path. Someday, I knew, I would die at her hands, as a destroyed plaything in the hands of a child. I felt like a snake-charmer, and a snake-charmer's hold over snakes is always tenuous, no matter how it looks. That fragile link can be broken at any moment. This is why so many snake-charmers die of snakebite.

The wariness, warranted as it was, did not last very long. The image of a raging demoness that I thought forever emblazoned in my mind, faded, overtaken by the intoxication of her presence. She was so loving, so joyful, so gently behaved. But a curtain had been lifted, and there was no turning away. Now, I could see that she was at no time wholly human. The way she approached the world, her judgements and ideas, these did not come from a place of humanity, rather from a kind of passionless vastness. I concluded that beings like her were not in any way at the level of human beings. Either they were above it, or below it.

One night she said, "In a few days, I'll take you very far away."

"Where?"

"That you'll find out."

"How far? In which direction?"

"So far, and in such a direction, that your mind cannot conceive of it. But, will your luck hold enough for you to be able to take the journey?"

Everything stood still as I registered the insinuation. The dark shadow of it felt like an ice-cold sliver of premonition from the demoness. But the demoness was nowhere in sight. Before me stood a young, exquisitely beautiful, intoxicating woman, brimming with love and joy. Goddesses are multitudes indeed, I thought, and whatever else she is, she is certainly a goddess.

Another day she said, "Trouble is coming for you, be prepared."

"What kind of trouble?"

"I'm not telling you that."

"Is my life in danger?"

"I'm not telling you that either."

"You protect me. I have nothing to fear."

"I can't stop this. No one can stop this. If it's coming for you, it's coming for you."

It came for me sooner than I thought.

At the three-month point, the people my family had hired to look for me arrived at that place. They reached the village first, where local people told them that there was a young man there, probably Bengali, and in the sad state of having lost his mind. They said he was always to be found alone sitting under a tree on the bank of the river, talking to himself in an undertone. Apparently, I had been spotted by the villagers on several occasions in this state.

They walked to the river to find that the reports were accurate. I was disheveled and filthy, my clothes were dirty and torn. It was clear that I had not taken care of myself in a while—I heard later that this is how they found me. They wanted to take me home at once, but I resisted strongly. That place held me firm, I would not leave. Looking back, I think I had truly taken leave of my senses, gone, or been driven insane. I would have found a way to make them leave and stayed on myself, but the goddess, my lover, she did not seem to want that.'

'What do you mean, she didn't want that?' I asked Taranath.

'They dragged me away from that place and locked me into a nearby cowshed. I found a way to escape at night, and dodged the guards to somehow make it back to my usual spot for a rendezvous with my lover, the goddess. "I will never leave you, or this place, ever again. This I swear," I told her passionately.

Her laugh was unkind. "This is not a situation of choice for you," she said. She said even a being of her power would not try to change the course of destiny. It was written that I would go, so I must leave. She knew that this was the last time that we would meet, never again. She said she had tried to prepare me by warning that something that could not be averted was coming for me. One does not ask a goddess how she knows such things, so I said nothing.

I returned home quietly, did whatever they told me to do. They said at home that someone had fed me a drug that had caused severe hallucinations and a complete break in connections with the world. I was treated in an insane asylum for a while, and got slowly better. Then, in a year or so, they decided on my marriage. I've been a householder ever since.'

***

'And you've never been tempted to pronounce those words, to call her again?' I insinuated carefully.

Taranath looked almost comically horrorstruck. 'What? No! You think inviting a goddess into your life is a game? She'll kill me the next time I call her! I would have to be extremely stupid to try that. In any case, this was a long time ago, a very long time ago.'

'Tell me truthfully, don't you feel like seeing her sometimes?'

The old man sat up, his face alight and flushed. 'Who said I don't want to see her? I told you, the three months I was with her were the only time in my life I felt truly alive, and complete, in my right place in the universe. She was a goddess, but came to me as a mortal. Her power so great that few could look at her and live. But when she was with me, she was a young woman of such grace, such charm, appealing little mannerisms and peals of crystal laughter—how could I forget things that my mind holds with such clarity?'

Taranath came out of the house to see me off. In the darkness of the street, he told me, 'We are so lonely, all of us, it's the human condition. Starved of love, always desperate, always searching for companionship. But you can't cut yourself adrift for that, you can't allow that to take over and drown everything else. No matter how hard it is, you must not waste your love on those who do not want it, those who value it lightly, or throw it away. So I will not call. But I am not happy and peaceful, do not think of me as peacefully settled in this life.'

'All I hear is that she gave you joy,' I said. 'I don't understand why you think that calling her destroyed your life.'

'It destroyed my life because I was never able to get joy from anything, ever again. It was as if those three months had used up all the happiness granted to me in this lifetime, and the rest of the years left are all turned to the same dull consistency as mud. I could never focus on anything enough to get better at it, couldn't settle anywhere. Sometimes I would feel like slowing down, but something or the other happened, and I moved restlessly on. I spent more time in an asylum, even after I was married. Then, years later, when I was finally better, I set up this small astrology business.

'I suspect that the skill I use for this work is a gift from the goddess. In that last conversation she had told me that I would never starve. I am grateful, my business does all right—well enough to keep us going. But that is not all one needs, is it?'

Taranath returned to the house, and I headed to Dharmatala. It felt wonderful to leave the strange, oppressive otherworld of night he had been describing, and find myself right in the middle of the twentieth century, with its lights and movement. I exhaled a deep breath of relief.

As long as Taranath told the story, I had been utterly absorbed in the strange events, and his telling of them, the expressions and tonalities. I did not think of the possible truth-value at all. As soon as I got on the tram car home, however, it struck me that—

Never mind. It doesn't matter.

OTHER TALES FROM THE SUPERNATURAL

Maya

Maya

It was two years ago. I still the remember broader events, although details have become fuzzy. Lots of memories feel confused.

Two years ago, I remember walking the road from Bogula towards Shidrani. I had just lost my job. I'd been working as a cook with a household at Bogula for about six years, now that job was gone.

I remember feeling bad about losing the job, but worse about the fact that I did not steal the butter they said I had. I did not know who had stolen it, but my employers decided it was me. So there I was, out on the road, walking. Shantipara and Sharashay passed in a frustrated, worried blur. By the time I crossed Bejerdanga it was well past noon and hunger had started gnawing at my belly. I was young and fit, but even though I had a little money, there were no shops open at that time in these remote areas.

Walking on at a much slower pace, I spotted a beautiful pond close to the road. It was still and peaceful, surrounded by old trees. I have always loved bathing surrounded by nature, so it didn't take much thought before I fell to this temptation. I stepped off the road, dropped my bag and clothes on the steps leading down to the water, and stepped right in. There were large clusters of water hyacinth and moss in the pool, it felt as if no one had used this side of the water for a long time. Carefully moving aside the weeds to make a nice-sized space of open water, I held my nose and let myself be completely submerged in the cool waters of the sheltered pond. The relief from the burning heat of mid-day summer was instant and complete.

I came out of the pond with my body cooled off, but my stomach rumbling loudly. Surely some of the trees in the woodland around would be in fruit in the summer? A first glance around told me that this was not the case, there was nothing to eat anywhere I could see.

Just as despair started to be added to the hunger gnawing at my stomach, I was distracted by an older man who also seemed to have come to the pond to cool off. He came up to me and asked, 'Where are you from?' I told him the truth—that I was a cook, a poor man looking for a job. But as of that moment I was extremely hungry, so did he know of any place nearby I could get something to eat?

The old man said, 'Wait a little bit, let me have a quick dip in the pond. I'll see to it that everything is all right for you.'

I waited by the side of the pond while the old man

bathed. Once he was done, I followed him on a path that led through a nearby village, then a forested area, into a big, old two-storeyed house. The old man introduced himself as we entered the house, 'My name is Nibarun Chakravarty. This is my house, but I don't live here. I live in Kolkata, in Shyambazar with my sons, who run a business there. This big old house is lying empty. Even when I visit, I use only use three rooms. Can you imagine how annoying it is that I have to come all this way once a month, simply because the house is lying empty? The fear of malaria keeps my sons away. This big house, the garden, all the trees are lying unused. I don't know who takes away the vegetables and fruit that grow on the property. Do you want to stay here?'

Taken a little aback at the suddenness of the offer, I responded with some caution, 'Yes, I could do that.'

'What work will you do?' He asked, completely ignoring the hesitation in my voice.

'I could cook,' I said, already beginning to settle into the idea.

'Yes, that's good. You cook for me the few days I'm here, and we'll both eat well.'

The old man seemed very pleased that I had accepted his offer. He had already cooked before leaving for his dip in the pond, so we shared what he had made for lunch. Afterwards, he gave me a comfortable mat and pillow and told me to get some rest.

I was exhausted after walking for hours in the heat. That, combined with the bath, the food, and a relaxation of both mind and body, meant that I slept all the way till late evening. The last weak rays of the day's sun were barely still touching the tops of the highest trees, and it was already dusk on the ground. I heard the calls of jackal start in the forest behind the house as I was waking up.

I came out of the room and started looking around. It seemed that the house was surrounded by trees in all directions. I spotted mango and jackfruit, but there were other kinds too. The property had evidently not been maintained for a while because the ground under the trees was densely covered in shrubbery that had grown quite high, with wild creepers festooned on both the shrubs and the tall trees. The effect was that of being closely surrounded by untouched forest. No other person or house was visible.

There was a small, decrepit room, not a part of the main house, but quite close to it. I peeked into this room, and found Nibarun Chakravarty leisurely smoking a water-pipe. He saw me and said, 'Do you know how to make tea? Then make tea, and fry some flattened rice. Let's have it with mustard oil, salt and green chillies.'

Once it was close to dinner time, he said, 'Put the rice on. We have the flavourful long-grained rice, and pure clarified butter. Boil some potatoes to go with that, and we're done.'

'As you wish.'

'You can make a vegetable dish for yourself if you like. Ridge gourd is growing wild behind the kitchen.

Take a lamp and go get as much as you want. And another thing, keep a lamp lit in the kitchen at all times.'

'I have to keep a lamp lit. How can I cook in the dark?'

'Yes, that's what I'm saying, keep it lit.'

While looking around earlier, I had realised how large the house was. The two floors of the house had fourteen or fifteen rooms, at my estimate, with open passages running the entire lengths in front of the rooms. All but two or three rooms were securely locked. The kitchen was fronted by a large open verandah that ran all the way to the nearest corner of the house. A few coconut trees and a grapefruit tree grew near this corner. In order to go behind the house and get to the gourd, I would have to walk to this edge of the open verandah, step down to the paved courtyard, walk through the yard, turn the next corner around the house, and walk a little further to be directly behind the kitchen and in the gourd-patch. My eyes had got used to the dark in my wanderings around the property, so I set off for the gourd-patch without a lamp. There was no need for one, I felt. Let the lamp stay in the kitchen.

The wild overgrowth of gourd plant behind the kitchen took me by surprise. It was clearly not a planting. The creepers had sprouted from the ground wherever seeds had randomly fallen, and kept growing immoderately. There was a wealth of ridge gourd on the plants. I started pushing aside the overgrowth and searching for the most tender gourds, the ones that would be sweetest when cooked.

I suddenly realised that there was someone else in the gourd patch with me. Peering through the vegetation, I saw a woman bending down to pick gourds, just like me. Her face was mostly covered, as would be normal for a woman of the village. I marked that others in the village seemed to be taking gourds from this patch, but didn't say anything.

I took my time to select a few tender gourds. When I was preparing to leave the patch and return to the kitchen, I glanced in her direction. She was still there, preoccupied in her task and seemingly unaware of my presence.

Once I was back, Nibarun Chakravarty asked, 'Did you find the gourd?'

'Yes, there was a lot of gourd growing wild. Another person was picking there too.'

He looked surprised. 'Where was there another person?'

'Behind the kitchen. In the dense part of the patch.'

'A man?'

'No, a woman.'

Chakravarty's face registered a curious combination of astonishment and annoyance. 'Where is this woman? Show this woman to me!' he demanded.

I took him around the house to the gourd patch, but she had gone.

'Where is she, then?' Chakravarty asked again.

'She was there a little while ago, just beside that deeper part of the thicket.'

'Humph. You're just saying whatever comes into your head! Seeing women in the daylight, really! Come on, enough of this nonsense, let's get back to the kitchen.'

I felt somewhat surprised at his reaction. Some wife or daughter of the village had come and picked a few gourds from a wild patch. Why was he getting so worked up about such a little thing? Besides, he had said that this house lay empty most of the time, that he was rarely here. Who did he expect to be guarding the patch of wild gourd when he was away?

It was peaceful until after dinner, when he abruptly brought the gourd-thievery up again. 'Why didn't you take a lamp with you to pick the gourd?' He asked suddenly, cutting through my thoughts which were elsewhere. 'Don't you remember that I told you to take a light with you when you went behind the kitchen? Why didn't you carry one?'

I genuinely did not understand why he was so upset with me. I had been able to see clearly in the half-light of dusk, so clearly in fact that I had spotted the woman stealing gourd, deep in the bushes. Perhaps the man's just a nag by temperament, I thought. Best to humour him.

'Keep a light with you at all times after dusk,' he said decisively.

'Why?' I was mildly annoyed at this high-handedness, but mostly curious.

'Because I say so. How old are you?'

'Thirty-seven or thirty-eight, I'm not sure.'

'I'm seventy-three. You're much younger than me. Listen carefully, and do exactly as I'm saying.'

'Yes, as you say.' I echoed dutifully.

Late that night, I was woken by loud sounds from the room above me. It felt as if large, heavy objects were being pushed and pulled around the room. I knew that the old man was due to leave for Kolkata the next day. He's probably packing, I thought. But so very late at night? And what a racket to make while packing to travel!

When I mentioned the noises to the old man the next morning, he looked startled. 'Me?' he said.

'Yes. Very late last night.'

'Oh. Yes…well…no… That's right…' he muttered, and walked away, with a distracted air.

'You could have told me, I would have helped,' I called after him. There was no answer.

By nine in the morning I had cooked rice, lentils and a fried gourd. He ate sparely, picked up his bags and headed for Kolkata. He was very kind before leaving. 'You must stay here as if this is your own home. There's guava, mango and jackfruit trees in the garden, and many more papayas than you could possibly use. A lot of land on the property is lying unused, plant anything you want on that land. Eat what you can, sell the rest. I have no need for any of it. Take care of the house as if it is yours. There's nothing to worry about. And another thing—'

'Yes?'

Suddenly sounding stern, he said, 'People will mock our arrangement. Pay no attention to them. Just take care of the house, and stay here as you will. Grow anything you need, take what you want off the trees, don't listen to anyone. I'm leaving two rooms unlocked for you.'

The old man went away. He left me feeling as if the heavens had opened up to let a windfall descend on my head. A few days ago I had been walking the road under burning summer skies with no prospect of a future. Now here I was in a huge house, with two large rooms open for my sole use. Besides that, a big verandah, the kitchen, the courtyard, a deep well placed just beside the house, so water was never going to be a problem. In addition to all these riches, the old man had left me with ten rupees, and a largish quantity of good quality long-grain rice. And the trees, so many trees, laden with fruit and vegetables to eat, and to sell. If this was not evidence of the blessings of a god, I did not know what else it could be.

Later that day, once the afternoon's heat had given way to the first cool evening breezes, I set out to find a provisions store in the village. Oil and salt were not available on the property, I would have to go out to buy them. Once out of the house in the daylight, I realised the true thickness of the forest surrounding the house. In fact it seemed as if the entire village was located inside a forest, which also freely entered the village at various points. The house was extremely isolated. I walked almost half a mile along narrow forest paths before meeting another person, a man. He, too, was on his way to buy oil. He asked me where I was staying.

'I'm staying at Nibarun Chakravarty's house.'

'That Chakravarty house? Why?'

'I'm the caretaker. I moved in yesterday.'

'You won't be able to stay in that house.'

'Why not?'

'I'm just saying that you won't be able to. Let's see what happens. So many people have tried to stay in that house, it hasn't worked. No member of the family has been able to stay in that house, let alone a complete stranger. In fact the younger people in the family don't even try to visit anymore.'

'Why is that?'

'I don't know. It's a terrible house in some way. You're not from around here, you'd better be very careful.'

The man said nothing further about the house. We did some small talk, and he bade me farewell and went on his way. I finished my work in the village and headed back home, feeling slightly uncomfortable about the conversation.

It was almost dusk by the time I got back. As I got closer to the house, I could see it looming through the jungle, two floors of quiet, squat, shut-down, opaque brick. The man was right, there was something strange about the house, something I didn't understand. The house looked curiously alive in the deepening dusk, as if it was sitting there in anticipation of something. Was it waiting to swallow a scrap of mortality, like me? For a moment, it felt as though my heart missed a beat.

No, there's nothing like that, I told myself sternly.

These jaundiced thoughts are not mine, they've been put there by that man and his insidious words. I was perfectly happy and at peace when I left the house to buy oil and salt, so why would I return just a few hours later to these unwanted thoughts and fears? What's wrong with that man, I fumed inwardly. To impose upon a total stranger in this thoughtless way—I had not asked his opinion about either the house, or my stay in it! How inconsiderate of him to inject such pointless fears into my head! But at least the old man had warned me that others may not like my guarding the property. I clearly remembered him saying that I was not to listen to anybody else's words, that I should stay in the house and take care of it as if it was my own.

It clicked into place. Of course, the people of the village did not want the property to be occupied. They had probably got into the habit of walking on to the grounds at any time, taking all the vegetables and fruits that grew in the orchards to eat, or sell in the market, just like the woman in the gourd patch last evening. My being on the property as a caretaker was a real obstacle to this access. Fear was a good way to get rid of me, and then the property would once again effectively belong to the village.

The truth was that I had never before lived in such comfort. The old man had asked of me no commitment to work, and there was no schedule to keep. An enormous property that I could use in any way I chose, and no work, except to cook my own basic meals. The rest of the time was to be used any way I chose. The freedom was intoxicating. Over the days, I fell into an uninterrupted routine of my own. The days were quiet, the nights quieter. I felt more carefree than I had in years.

One of those evenings, I had finished cooking my simple dinner and was sitting on the verandah in front of the kitchen, singing to myself. Sitting on the verandah and singing was well on its way to becoming a favourite part of my daily routine. Suddenly, the strangest thing happened. Water started flowing from a drain-spout on the upper floor. The stream of water landed on the ground floor gutter almost right in front of me, so I was certainly not imagining it. It felt exactly as if someone was thoroughly washing their hands and feet at the draining point on the upper balcony, and the water was following the slope through the drain-spout to the gutter directly below. The stream of water was thin, but it fell continually with no breaks.

I stepped down to the garden and tried to peer up to the top floor balcony. Everything there looked shut-down and quiet, as it usually did. Then I went to the other side of the house to check on the access stairs to the top floor. The old man had locked the door to those stairs and taken the key with him. The door was still securely bolted and padlocked. The upper floor was not possible for me, or for anyone else to reach. Where, then, was all that water coming from?

The drain stopped running in about ten minutes. By then, I had worked out a logical reason for the otherwise inexplicable flow. The old man must have forgotten a pitcher or pot of water on that part of the balcony. It would have been full, and may have tipped over, or broken. I became convinced that I was correct in my reasoning. After all, what else could be the cause of so much water?

Nighttime came on, and worn out from all the excitement and speculation in my otherwise eventless life, I went to bed early. I must have fallen asleep as soon as my head hit the pillow, because the next thing I remember is opening my eyes to the beautiful sight of full moonlight streaming in through the window and falling across my bed. A fragrant flower was blooming somewhere, I could smell it clearly—

What flower? asked a quiet, but distinct part of my still-waking mind. There were no fragrant plants on this side of the house.

I was off the bed before the thought was complete. Where was that fragrance coming from? My eyes were drawn to the brightest thing in the room, which was the window. As I glanced at the window, I saw a woman pass it as if she had stepped up to the verandah in front of my room, and was now headed to the corner of the house with the coconut trees. I saw her clearly, and I have no problems with my vision.

Hurrying to the door, I opened it and walked out onto the verandah. The sweet smell was still there, but fainter, as if the woman had wafted it in her wake. Now that she was gone, it had immediately started to fade. But I could still smell it, and it didn't smell like any flower I knew. It felt familiar, somehow, but unclassifiable.

I was feeling a little strange, a little drunk from the sweetness of the alien perfume. And where was she, the woman who had walked past my window? Barely a moment had passed between my seeing her through the window and rushing out onto the verandah, which was quite long. I ran to the corner near the coconut trees and looked around, but she had left no trace, except the fragrance that could have only come from her. It ebbed away into nothingness as I stood there, confused and slightly alarmed. There was nothing else to be done, that night. I retired slowly to my room, and slept peacefully until late morning.

I awoke contented and refreshed. Thinking over the odd events of the night before, I decided that it was a decidedly odd and vivid dream. Perhaps my mind, longing for company, had made up a mysterious woman to visit me in this place of absolute solitude where no one else ever came. I wished that this house was not quite so distant from other homes. It would have been wonderful to hear the sound of other voices, perhaps a family going about their regular day as I went about mine. But the house was so remote from other houses, and separated by such dense greenery, that I may as well have been the only person left in the world. The loneliness, I reflected, was proving more difficult than I had thought it would be.

Another strange thing happened that afternoon.

The rice had just finished boiling, and I was doing the minor balancing act needed to drain the starch, when laughter rang out from the balcony on the upper floor. It wasn't the kind of laughter one may expect in a relatively remote location—not like, say, one person laughing at something that had amused them—but many harsh, bass voices laughing together, the sound cutting sharp and clear through the still, hot afternoon. The volume and quality of the laughter made it impossible to ignore. It sent an involuntary shiver through my entire body, I almost lost my grip on the pot. I put it down carefully, and ran out beyond the verandah in front of the kitchen to stare in disbelief at the balcony on the upper floor.

It was utterly and completely empty, and quiet. The windows and doors to the rooms beyond were securely shuttered, as they had been since the old man left. Bizarre laughter still ringing in my ears, I ran around the other side of the house to the door which led to the upper floor. It was still padlocked, exactly as it had been when I last checked. It was daylight, so I felt quite disturbed, but not fearful. It is hard to feel afraid of bogeymen when the skies are clear and blue, and the sun is shining bright. If I had heard that booming, knife-edged, utterly outlandish laughter at night, I think my response would have been more immediate and visceral. I would have fallen into some kind of a terrified, jaw-clenched unconsciousness. Whoever found me would have had to prise my teeth open with the flat part of a key.

I returned shakily to the kitchen, and slowly put the gourd on to cook. I remembered how much gourd I had, as master of this entire property. Gourd, and so much else, all mine to do with as I wish. No poor man had ever before had such riches at his disposal. I must keep that at the top of my mind.

I continued my routine, ears alert for any disturbance from the upstairs balcony. It was entirely peaceful and silent. No people, no laughter, not even the scratching sounds of a mouse. Somewhat less apprehensive, I lay down on my bed for a nap. In a waking doze, I dreamed that I was in a large gathering of people. People were talking, laughing, moving around me, while I continued sleeping amidst them. I could hear their voices, but not the details of what they said. Perhaps the whole thing was a construction of my isolated, fevered mind, I half-thought, as one sometimes does in dream. Perhaps the laughter, too, was some kind of extension of the dream-world. Perhaps that earlier vivid dream had led to this one, with the many gathered people.

Nine eventless days passed.

The human mind is a strange thing. It tries to rid itself of unpleasantness as quickly as possible, and it sometimes succeeds quite well. As the tranquil days passed, I explained to myself that it was all just nothing. There was nothing to be worried about at all. The woman passing my window at night was a figment of my imagination, as was that horrible otherworldly laughter. Deprived of social contact, it was all simply a playing out of the dramatic and rich parts of my overactive imagination.

I became quite healthy and contented over those nine days. Having no work responsibilities suited me just fine. I had always seen myself as a busy, energetic, active person, but now it was as if my body and mind loosened and relaxed. I had worked very hard from quite a young age, and it seemed that now, given the chance, I just wanted to sleep and eat.

On the evening of the ninth day, I felt that perhaps I had rested enough. It was now time to work on some of the improvements I had been planning. The priority was to clean up the mess of overgrowth in which the gourd plants were drowning—while keeping the gourd creepers safe of course. I had noticed a pumpkin plant starting in the wild abandon of that patch. After cleaning out the weeds, I would lay a roped link from the base of that plant to the roof of the first floor, and wrap the pumpkin creeper along that line, so its future growth would be upwards and away from the ground. It would be a joy to do gardening work in this house. All the needed tools were stored where I could easily access them, and had clearly been well maintained.

I headed for the gourd patch and started working, head down and focused on getting the weeding done as soon as possible. It felt good to be absorbed in doing something productive again. About half an hour later, I happened to glance towards the denser part of the patch and realised that I was not alone. There was a woman in that further part of the gourd patch, and like the last time, she was bending down to pick gourds from the stems closer to the ground.

Two things happened very close together. My mind registered the woman in the patch, and that horrible laughter started up from the upper floor of the house. This time I heard a hubbub behind the laughter, as if there was a large number of people on the upper floor, and they were whispering and giggling behind the demoniac laugh. Then, I clearly heard all the shutters of the upper floor doors and windows being blown open at once, as if the space was no longer able to hold some uncontrollable force.

Heart leaping in my chest, I ran to the yard to be able to see as much of the upper floor as possible. How could such a thing have happened? What was I to do, now?

But all was quiet again. The balcony was empty and still, all the doors and windows were tightly shuttered and closed. What, exactly, was wrong with this house? It brooded most of the time, tightly wrapped in a shroud of absolute eventless silence. And sometimes it would shake with these frightful convulsions, peopled with invisible talkers and laughers. And the woman, picking gourd in the din. What sense was I supposed to make of this periodic madness?

Another strange thing happened later that night.

I was lying on my bed, half-asleep. Suddenly, something alerted me, and my eyes sprang open. I saw there were many people around my bed. They were all wearing celebratory turbans in red, and they carried short sticks. But this was not the strangest thing. The strangest thing was that they looked exactly alike, all the faces and bodies were the same. It was as if I was seeing about fifty carbon-copies of one man in my dozing state. They had another commonality—None of them even glanced in my direction.

One spoke, 'Somebody seems to be present among us today.'

Another responded, 'A man of the earth has a house here for a long time. I have not seen the house, but I have heard it spoken of. Those who can see such things have seen it. Another man has come to live in that house.'

A third voice, 'All lies. Where is this house?'

A fourth voice, 'None of us have seen it.'

The first voice again, 'Come, then, let us dance.'

Disbelieving, I saw the fifty or so identical people in that suddenly-enormous room break into a riotous, yet seemingly structured dance. They danced in a large loose circle, a part of which passed right through my bed, and me. Loud drums were playing a strange percussive rhythm, and all the dancers kept it perfectly. It was clear that they were entirely oblivious to my presence. I could see them, yet did not feel even the faintest physical sensation as they danced and jumped and whirled, around, and right through me, repeatedly. I got dizzy and my head began to spin, but I kept watching this outlandish scene as long as I could. I lost consciousness at some point. The last I remember, the drums were still playing that odd beat, and they were still dancing.

I woke from the unconscious state in the very early dawn. The last of the moonlight lay peacefully across my bed, and that remembered sweet fragrance of the unknown flower filled the cool early-morning air. Strangely content, I lay there watching through the window as dawn broke among the trees. Sleep must have overtaken me, because I awoke properly later in the morning.

While getting off the bed, I realised that I felt very well rested, as if I had spent a long uninterrupted night in deep sleep. I felt fit and healthy and ready to start the day, exactly as one feels after a night of complete rest. If I had slept restfully through the night, who, then, had seen the ghost-dance? Those dancers had hopped, stepped, and whirled through my body and face. Was that a dream? What about the fragrance in the cool of the early morning, the sweetness that the woman wafted when she was around? I had not been the slightest bit dizzy when I smelt that, in fact it still lingered in my memory—I could smell it if I tried.

Maybe that was some unknown night-blooming wildflower. After all, I was a stranger to these parts. Who knows what wildflowers may bloom at night, and droop away during the harsh light of day? Yes, a wildflower. That must be it.

I went to the village provisions store to buy oil. The woman minding the shop asked, 'So, how are you doing? Have you seen anything?'

'No.'

'Have you heard anything?'

'No.'

'Very good, you're safe then. The men who stayed in that house before you would quite frequently see a woman. All kinds of other things would happen. I don't know what effect these things had, but gradually they would stop leaving the house altogether. They would starve themselves, get thinner and thinner, and then eventually die in the house. This is what happened with the two men that tried to stay in that house, before you came. That house is a bad place, ghosts gather there, we all know that. Ghosts can drive people completely mad. The men before you stopped eating, or moving around, they just lay in the house until they died, couldn't leave it and go away, couldn't even go too far from it. Looks like you're comfortable there, that's good I guess. In the village, we know better than to venture anywhere near that house.'

Walking back, I mulled over what she had said. Could that be happening to me? Were the ghosts starting to make me lose my sanity, my moorings in the world? Could ghosts actually do that to the living?

But as soon as I got nearer to the house, my misgivings vanished. All was good. I'm happy and content here. Where should I go, if I left? I had nowhere else to be. I'm in excellent health, and a peaceful state of mind. There would be no point at all in leaving.

It's been two years since that conversation. I live in the house. The old man had promised me a small wage, but he has not sent anything in this time. That doesn't bother me. I look after the house, eat what the garden grows, watch them dance at night. You could say that I live with them. I don't remember when I last left the house. Why should I go anywhere? Everything I need is right here.

An Open Door

Khola dorjar itihaash

SANTOSH DUTTA WAS a son-in-law of our village. He didn't live in these rural parts, just came in about once a week to check on his wife's property. She was an only child, so the husband and wife were to inherit everything that her father owned. This is how he was known to us. But in Kolkata where he lived, he was known to be an expert in the afterlife. So much of an expert, in fact, that he was often called by clubs and societies to give talks on the subject.

To our mutual satisfaction, Santosh was also an accomplished storyteller. We would invite him to our gatherings when he visited. There would be hot tea and snacks, and he would tell us about strange happenings and ideas to which we thrilled, but also treated with a measure of disbelief.

At the time of the events in this story, a gentleman called Ram Chakravarty lived in the local teacher's hostel in our village. He taught science and logic at the village school and was a regular at our little get-togethers. Ram was a sceptic to his bones.

'Can you prove that there is an afterlife?' He demanded of Santosh one evening, when the latter was halfway through a story.

'No,' returned Santosh, with equal belligerence. 'There is no room to prove anything here, but I can tell you about all these things that have happened—'

'Yes, tell me, what things have happened?'

'But, better than that—'

'Do you personally believe in this nonsense?'

'Yes, I do.'

'How did you come to know about the afterlife?'

'Knock, and the door will be opened unto you.'

'All this is very vague talk.'

'Nobody has been able to be more specific than this in conversation. I can't prove the afterlife while sitting here and drinking tea with you. It would be better if I could bring Rekha here, and she could bring down the afterlife and show it to you.'

'Who is Rekha?'

'She's a medium, and very good at it. Our Psychic Society is so impressed that we pay her enough retainer to run her entire household.'

'How old is she?'

'About seventeen or eighteen. She has astonishing ability. Several disbelievers have joined our Society after seeing what she can do. But unfortunately, we may have to soon let go of her.'

'Why?'

'She's a medium for spirits, like an open window. Various kinds of spirits from the afterlife treat her as a channel. They enter her once the window is open. Not all of those spirits are good.'

'What do you mean, "enter her"?'

'She's a medium. So when she opens the window to her being, spirits come and enter her physically. They possess her. Of late, it seems like too many bad spirits know about her window, they are making it very difficult for her to keep being a medium.'

'What a strange fairy tale this is.'

'You're an educated person. What is proof for you? Is it seeing something with your own eyes—what do your books of logic say? Would you trust as proof something you experience for yourself? Come with me then. 67 Nandanbagan Street, that's the small house in which Rekha and her family live. But just because the Psychic Society pays her rent, we can't ask her to give herself up entirely, martyr herself to her skill. Very soon, she will have nothing of herself left, everything will be yielded to the other world.'

'What does that mean?'

'I've been trying to tell you what it means, but you're not listening. What this means is that in the worst case scenario, one of the spirits that enter her though the open window will take over, and drive Rekha out of her own body.'

All the arguments of the teacher of logic fell apart at

this blatant fabrication of pure impossibility. Ram leaned back in his chair and started to laugh. 'See, this is why people like me find it so difficult to believe people like you. Please, go on, I'm listening.'

But Santosh had other plans. 'Oh no,' he said, 'No more talk. I'll take you to Nandanbagan street, and you can see for yourself. Nothing I say will be able to convince you better than that.'

While approving of direct proof, Ram still wanted to listen to the full story. 'Yes, that will be good, I'd like to go there,' he said. 'Now please go on and tell us what happened next.'

Slightly mollified, Santosh continued, 'A few days ago, her mother was at home when Rekha came to her and said, "Sister, you didn't even perform the death-rituals for me. Go to Gaya and complete my death-rituals. Only good can come to you if you do that." Suspecting her daughter was possessed by a spirit again—as has frequently happened lately—Rekha's mother kept her composure. "Who are you?" she asked. Rekha said, "I'm Parul, from Hemnagar."

'Rekha's mother guessed, "It's been a while since you died, Parul!" Rekha was undeterred. "Yes, I'm dead, so what? I come to your house everyday, I go to Hemnagar, sometimes I visit my older sister at her in-law's house in Sodhpur. Moving around is no problem for me now. I have no pain, no worries. The only problem is that I can't go on to the next stage. Something holds me here. That's why I want you to finish my death-rituals, so that I can move on." She paused for a few seconds, and then continued, "Ok, I'd better go. There's a woman here, she wants my place in Rekha's body. I'll go and chase her off."

'Alarmed at this new development, Rekha's mother asked, "Who is she?"

"She used to visit my area. I think her moral character is not very good. She killed herself, and now she's in pain."'

The implication of this comment was not lost to the scientist in Ram. 'Just a moment,' he said, 'what do you mean, her moral character is not good? What does that mean in the afterlife? There are moral standards after death? I need an answer to this question before we go on!'

'We are the same, before and after death,' replied Santosh Dutta. 'Nobody intervenes from outside and changes our personality after we die. In death, as in life, these things are all in our own minds. But this is irrelevant—let me complete the story. Sometimes mischievous spirits enter Rekha's body. They make her talk in languages that she does not know, such as Oriya and Hindi. Once she was possessed by a European woman who claimed that she lived in the Park Circus area of Kolkata when she was alive. When that possession happened, Rekha spoke fluent English. But she knows no language other than Bangla.'

'And you have seen and heard this yourself?' asked Ram in a tone of total disbelief.

'Of course I have, didn't you hear what I was saying? I've also heard her speak fluent Oriya, another language she doesn't know. And that's not the point either. The point is that the strangest, and worst, that can happen is that mean or low spirits from the afterlife possess her while the window is open.'

'Why? What do they do?'

'They make all kinds of trouble for Rekha's body. They fling her to the ground, or make her stay out in the afternoon sun for hours. One time, she kept trying to burn herself. There is a particular danger from those beings known in English as elementals—those are the worst, always hellbent on making mischief, doing as much damage as they can. The only blessing when dealing with elementals is that they do not have any physical form by themselves, and so they cannot touch things of the material world.'

'Such utterly nonsensical stories on this rainy evening.'

'Aren't you coming with me to Nandanbagan?'

'I may well do that.'

'Is there a problem with coming to see for yourself?'

'No, no problem at all. Let's take the bus and go to Nandanbagan tomorrow.'

This is how Ram Chakravarty, teacher of mathematics and logic, started on a path that was to end with his death. The newspapers reported wrongly on his death, and even the police investigators did not arrive at the correct conclusions. Rekha was responsible, certainly, but not in the way they thought. She was not that kind of girl at all.

Exactly nine days after this conversation, on a full-moon holiday, a few of us met in the evening and followed Santosh to Nandanbagan street.

Rekha's place was small and tucked away in a narrow lane. You entered the house through a side-door that led to a small open space. Beyond the open space were two rooms of moderate size, and behind those two rooms was another much smaller room with a tiny balcony beyond it. Perhaps the balcony was originally intended as a kitchen, since it had a stove built into the floor. At the time we went there, it held only a few potted plants and a tricycle belonging to Rekha's youngest brother.

Rekha brought us tea. She was darkish, small, nice-looking in an unremarkable way. She had strange eyes, they seemed both empty and wide-open. The blank innocence of those eyes felt odd on an almost-grown woman. Santosh Dutta told her, 'Today I have brought our friend Ramlal Chakravarty. You'll have to show him what you can do.'

Rekha said, 'Something has been giving me a really hard time for a few days now. I can't make out if it's human or animal, but it feels powerful. It may come again today. I'm scared of it.'

Once it was dark, Rekha's mother led us to the small room at the back. It had been arranged with incense and flowers. We sat around a table. The lights were dimmed, and a record with shehnai music was put on the gramophone.

There was a soft sound from a corner of the room, like someone whispering. We couldn't make out the words. Santosh said—'who is speaking?'

The voice got a little louder. It was a woman's voice. It said, 'Don't let Rekha sit in the circle today.'

'Why should we listen to you? Who are you?'

'I am Rekha's aunt, her father's sister, Niradabala. She is not well today, and there are bad things waiting for her to open the window.'

'Are you still here?'

There was silence, she was gone.

Time went by. It was so pitch dark in the room that the air seemed to become heavier. Rekha was absolutely quiet, so quiet in fact that she fell asleep, and we could hear her gentle snoring. She was still sleeping, when someone spoke through her mouth. We knew it wasn't her because of the low, gravelly male voice—'Malati, o Malati—'

Santosh said, 'Who are you? Malati has not come here today.'

'I'm her husband. When she comes, tell her that I'm looking for her. But tell the medium to get up, now. There is great danger today.'

'What danger?'

Rekha went quietly back to snoring. More time passed. We sat around the table in the almost total lack of light and sound, while the night grew later. Nobody came. Maybe half an hour more passed in utter silence. I was just thinking that it was perhaps best to let it go for the day, and that everyone needed to get home, when there was a very small sound from the corner of the room. It was a suppressed little sound, but we all heard it clearly. The air in the room started feeling heavy again, but this time there was a distinct chill to it. Santosh Dutta did not get up and move away, as he had been on the verge of doing. Taking his cue, we all kept sitting.

I could not see anyone else in the dark. Suddenly, I felt as if someone had set down a basket full of ice on my head. Then, someone reached down from above, and started blocking my nostrils. It became difficult to breathe. It felt as if they had installed an ice-making machine in the room, and it just kept churning out ice and heavy, thick air, it would not stop. My breathing became shallower, feeling disappeared from my hands and feet.

Rekha whimpered in the dark. It sounded like a suppressed sound of pain and fear.

There was no other sound that reached my ears, I could not see anything. Yet it felt as if there was a factory in that little room with me, busy people bustling around, the hum and hustle of things in progress, getting ready for—

'Put the lights on,' said Santosh suddenly. 'Put the lights on at once, look that thing—'

Even through the darkness, there was something darker in the room. It looked like a shadow on the wall. It looked like the shadow of a man. No, it had the rough shape of a man, but distorted, like a shadow you may have seen as a child in the depths of a dense grove of bamboo in the late dusk of a monsoon evening, the air heavy and still. It looked like it had no eyes or ears or nose, flatness where there should be contour.

The air became colder still, and I slipped into a semi-conscious state. I no longer knew where I was. Somewhere in a deep, dark forest, a powerful being, a demon, was wrapped in meditation that longed for the destruction of human lives and homes. The demon was dumb, it had no language. Perhaps it did not have a mouth. It had a gaze of intense cruelty and violence, but it had no eyes. That thing was no human. It was also nothing like any picture of a ghost, devil or demon, or any other supernatural being that I had ever seen. Nothing I had ever seen before in reality, image, imagination, or dream came anywhere close to that thing.

The shadow on the wall started growing, like a mushroom, or a shadow of a man moving forward. In the dark, I could see it getting wider, and taller and bigger and somehow more dense, and slowly starting to take up more and more space. It was trying to take up all the space in the room, it was coming closer and closer, and soon it would touch me. The dark, dense shadow, getting bigger like a child's balloon, but saturated with a sense of cruelty, rage, and evil that was a physical thing in the room, nobody was going to survive this—

There was a scream in the room, it was cut off abruptly. The shadow was spreading faster, it was close to taking over the room, it had spread over us already, now it was much bigger than the room, it was going to cover everything, it wanted to swallow anything it crossed.

The soft waxy thing which had earlier blocked my nostrils, now climbed down and was in front of me. I clearly felt it completely closing up more and more of my face—my mouth, my nose, my eyes. I stopped being able to speak, and then I stopped being able to breathe. Somewhere, a clock struck one. Two. Three. Four. Five. Six. Seven. Eight. Nine. Ten.

It was ten o'clock. That was the last thing I remember before I entirely lost consciousness.

The next thing I remember is opening my eyes slowly. It was still night, but the room was no longer dark. The windows were now open, and the moon lay across the floor of a part of the room. The others were still unconscious, lying slumped in their chairs, eyes shut, limbs relaxed and askew. Santosh Dutta was missing. I tried to exert some control over my sluggish thoughts, and my short-term memory revived first. Where was the fearsome shadow? I clearly remembered Rekha sitting in the circle as a medium just after dusk. It was completely dark then, all the windows had been tightly closed and latched. How was there moonlight in the room? The careless shapes of the unconscious people in reflected moonlight looked as if the room had been the scene of a gruesome murder. I heard the distant motor of a car, coming closer.

Very soon after his, Santosh Dutta entered the room. He had brought a doctor.

Everyone around the table was restored to consciousness. Everyone, that is, except Ram Chakravarty. He had died a while ago. The doctor said he had died of asphyxiation, that the air had run out for him. His face was dark, and he showed all the other physical signs of asphyxiation, so the diagnosis was not challenged. The police came and said that it could be some gas that stops the lungs from breathing, but the only gas they found was the household variety, used for cooking. People from the neighbourhood came to huddle and gossip.

I next met Santosh Dutta a long time after this episode. By then, the vividness of the events in that room had faded enough in my mind that I was able to ask him for an explanation for the strange events of that evening.

'No one would have survived, that evening,' he said. 'The earlier spirit warned us to be careful. We should have listened.'

'Two spirits did that,' I said. 'Rekha's aunt, and Malati's husband.'

'It wasn't a spirit at all, mischievous or otherwise,' he said. 'It was far more powerful than any spirit. Rekha's aunt called it a thing. She was right. It was a particular type of very powerful supernatural being, in English they call it an elemental. They are like the apex predators of the animal world, think of tigers or bears in the wild. But they are not just blindly powerful, they are also intelligent, and extremely cunning. The one that came that day had a particular plan. It wanted to become a part of the physical, tangible, material world—having corporeality would make it many times more powerful. So it tried to steal our materiality from us, to suck up not our minds or souls, but our bodies. It was planning to use the matter that makes us, fashion that matter to its own needs, and fully enter our world.

'But I blame myself, how stupid and slow I became in that room. I could have stopped it, I could have put an end to it before the bad things happened.'

'How?' I asked. This was certainly something important to know.

'By turning on the light. Just getting up and pressing the switch. When the dark vanishes, fear, sprits, elementals, everything vanishes. You should always put on the light before it gets bad. I don't know why I didn't, that night. I'll always blame myself.'

The Curse

Obhishaap

'THIS IS *THAT* Pratap Narayan Choudhury's house.'

I stared at the crumbling pile of brick and stone. This was the fabled Pratap Narayan Choudhury mansion? It was difficult to believe.

The last light of day still lingered in the western sky, but darkness was close. The last birds were flying homeward, their calls mingling with the wind and filling the dusk. We could hear the strength of the Ganga's current, rushing onward to an unseen confluence. Surrounded by the omnipresent peace and beauty of this part of the country, I stood looking at the famous cursed house of Pratap Narayan Choudhury.

It stood on the bank of the river, almost completely covered in creepers and the absolute stillness that takes over once human life retreats. Waning light reflecting off the river cast eerie trembling shadows on the broken remains of what was once a palatial building. It felt as if all that was left of past glories were the skeletal remains of the palace, and the ghosts of the people who once lived there. Everything else had floated down the river to invisibility and insignificance. Nature had arranged the remains with her own hands—sculpted human arrangements of grandness and status, given way to careless, living, wild green beauty. A small boat with a single boatman rowed slowly home, the song of the boatman wafting to us in the evening gloom. It was the only human voice we could hear, seemingly the only sign of other humanity in this world, slowly leaching colour into the grayscale towards dark.

Everybody knew of Pratap Narayan Choudhury of Palashpur. His lordship had left Palashpur rigid with fear. No one dared disobey him. It was said that his absolute control extended to the animal kingdom, and that tigers and cows would drink water side-by-side without dispute during his rule. Even in those days, there were very few local lords with as much power as he wielded.

The Choudhury family's influence was closely tied with the rise of the British. The zamindari of Palashpur had been awarded to Dhurjyoti Narayan Choudhury by British overlords in appreciation of the numberless services, of all kinds, that he had rendered over the years. Dhurjyoti Narayan was the first of Palashpur's Choudhury lords.

The soldiers of his son, Bijoy Narayan Choudhury, played a leading role in the British suppression of the sepoy rebellion at its source, Barrakpore. Captain

Lawrence and his family managed to escape the wrath of the revolt under Bijoy Narayan's protection. History has not recorded this incident, but everybody knows about it. The fact is, at the end of March 1957, when the skies were dark with danger and fear, Dhurjyoti Narayan was at Barrakpore, ever of service to his masters. Later, after it was all over and the British had won, Lawrence presented Bijoy Narayan with a scabbarded sword as a token of his loyalty. This gift was revered by the family as a symbol of their honour and pride, and it was prominently displayed in the Choudhury house for a long time.

But let us return to the present for a moment before we get into the heart of the story. I had come across the famously cursed Palashpur zamindari house while on summer vacation. My friend Kamal Haldar invited me along to his home at Beledanga, and we were out enjoying an evening walk along the Ganges when we came upon the decaying remains of what must have been in its time a magnificent and palatial building. Kamal said, 'This is *that* Pratap Narayan Choudhury's house.'

Like many others, I had heard stories of the fearsome, legendary patriarchs of the Choudhury clan. The utterly broken-down shell of the famous zamindar house left me speechless. It was clear to me that no one had lived there in a long time, that it had been completely given over to the encroaching wilderness.

Bijoy Narayan's son, Pratap Narayan, oversaw the pinnacle of Choudhury glory. But just as Pratap Narayan saw the meteoric rise of the family's fortune, he was also privy to the beginnings of its eventual decline. In this, Pratap Narayan was like the Mughal emperor Aurangzeb, who also saw the rise and the fall of the fortunes of his line in his own lifetime. The aged emperor eventually died of grief far away, in the south. But here is the difference. Where Aurangzeb was principled and religious, Pratap Narayan was the exact opposite. As the stories I heard tell it, the two factors most responsible for the family's decline during his time were unspeakably bad moral character, and a tendency to get involved in multiple complicated legal entanglements.

There was no space for ethics or principles in Pratap Narayan's vision of the world. He was principally interested in alcohol and women, and the little time left over from dissolute pursuits he devoted to contesting vicious legal battles. Very few people of his era could argue in court like him, although he had almost no other familiarity with the form of the law, or indeed formal education in general.

It was said that his actual specialization was bringing unhappiness to women. No one knew how many women had wept, hopeless and unheard, on how many dark nights, in the entertainment hall of that massive house. Perhaps his conquering laughter and their frantic tears still echo somewhere in a shadow of that dire space, now held in place only with crumbling brick and rock.

He married a woman named Khiradasundari, and romanced her widowed sister, Abhamoyee. It was made clear that Khiradasundari had no right to protest. Abhamoyee was very young and recently a widow. She succumbed to the lure of possible love, and the pressure Pratap Narayan put on her to give in to his desires. But eventually, unable to deal with the wrenching disapproval of family, and the larger society of Palashpur, she killed herself.

Pratap Narayan stopped meeting his wife after Abhamoyee's death. Over the next few years, Khiradasundari continued living in that house with her son, as far away from her husband's attention as possible.

Meanwhile, Pratap Narayan's behaviour became even more reckless and degenerate, and his hatred for women assumed monstrous proportions. He blamed women for the troubles in his life, justifying his worsening actions as revenge on the society that had mistreated Abhamoyee and driven her to suicide. But what he actually did was set fire to whatever peace his subjects had enjoyed up to that time.

The daughters and wives of Palashpur became the new objects of his predatory hunger. He would roam the fields and forests all day with his gun, shooting birds. In the evening he would return to this house, through the town. The path he took to return home became the bane of the women in Palashpur. No girl or woman was safe on that path if they caught Pratap Narayan's eye. At that time, there were no colonial laws against this kind of violent kidnapping.

Pratap Narayan had a henchman called Blind Kalu.

He was blind in one eye, most likely as a result of some act of depraved violence in the past. But what he lacked by way of vision, he made up with base cunning, and a joy in the use of the power granted to him by his master. He terrorized people with his henchmen to keep the rule of his master's arbitrary laws, and he was the one who kept Pratap Narayan's deviant appetites satisfied. It was said with bitterness that with Blind Kalu around, his master need have no fear of going hungry at all.

One particular night of high winds and raging storm, Kalu returned to the palace bringing with him an unknown woman kidnapped for his master. It was about ten o'clock, and a hard rain was falling in blinding sheets. The wind was relentless, it moaned and shrieked through the night like some enormous disembodied being mourning an irreparable loss.

Pratap Ranjan was lining his eyes carefully with lamp-black in anticipation of the evening's entertainment, when Kalu walked soundlessly into the room.

'Maharaj.'

'Oh, you're back!'

'She's here.'

'Tell her to rest. How far has she come?'

'Almost thirteen miles.'

'How is she?'

'Fit to receive your blessing.'

'Good.'

Pratap Narayan finished his toilette and hurried to the entertainment hall of his mansion. He found the woman in a far corner of the large room, huddled into a niche in the wall. She was shivering and crying quietly, soaked through, her clothes torn and dirtied. Misery was written in every line of her body. Bruises that were still darkening on her skin showed that she had fought to get away.

The motion of Pratap Narayan's entrance made her look up, a flash of hope lighting her face. It was very brief. As soon as she realised who it was that had come for her, she pulled herself deeper into the shallow niche, her throat producing a sound that was purely primal fear.

Pratap Narayan's many power-hungry, debased appetites looked at the helplessly weeping woman on his floor and felt a powerful surge of excitement. He moved close to her and asked as gently as he could, 'What is your name?'

She said nothing, so he moved closer. 'Do you see this huge mansion? This limitless wealth? This is all yours. Tonight, you are my queen.'

She looked up from her sunken misery, tears running down her face. 'No, no, I don't want to be a queen. I am not a queen. I am a beggar, please, let me stay a beggar. I beg you, I fall at your feet, please send me back to my husband and child.' She fell at Pratap Narayan's feet and held onto them as if they were the only thing in the world that could save her.

His laughter echoed through the empty hall. 'That's impossible!' he declared, and the sound of that declamation filled the huge room to the rafters. He had decided that this was one of the most flawlessly beautiful women he had ever seen. He wanted to possess her completely, in every way he could. Her tearful pleas sounded honeyed to his ears, her words only whetted his appetite.

Maybe it was the laughter, but there was a sudden, almost imperceptible shift in the atmosphere. Her tone changed. She sat up and looked straight at him. Her face was flushed and bruised, still damp with tears. 'Let me go,' she said. 'It will be better for you, if you let go.'

Pratap Narayan laughed again, this time genuinely amused. 'What could I possibly stand to gain from *you*?' he said, entertained at the mere possibility that she could benefit him in any way.

She cut him off before he could go on.

'You will be destroyed,' she said, in a voice that sounded like shards of glass. 'It will all be over for you. My curse will burn all this, your grand home, to the ground. There will be nothing left.'

A completely unexpected sliver of fear snaked up Pratap Narayan's back. He hesitated in his tracks. There was a pause, a moment of quiet. Her voice, now utterly composed, cut through the silence. 'If I have been a good woman in my life, you will never be able to stand against my curse. You, your family, your descendants, everybody will be ruined.'

Pratap Narayan was utterly taken aback that a woman entirely under his control could curse him in this unmistakably definite and arrogant manner. But his initial flash of disquiet had been overtaken by resolution to stay his course, and the ability to see the links between actions and consequences had never been one of his strengths. He heard the woman's words, but did not listen to them. This was to be the last hunt of his life.

The next day, an almost-imperceptible pall of gloom settled over the mansion. It felt like a subtle poison in the air. The woman was still on the premises, and rumours from the kitchen said that she wasn't eating or drinking at all. Already starved for two days after she was kidnapped—the time it had taken to get her to Palashpur and Pratap Narayan—the continuing hunger strike took her toward serious deterioration.

She had also stayed entirely quiet, not answering questions or saying anything herself. Unable to tolerate the way she silently stared at him, and unaccustomed to the beginnings of a deep fear he did not quite understand, Pratap Narayan left the house and went away. Shortly after, Khiradasundari emerged from her longtime solitude. She went to meet the woman in a part of the mansion that she had always considered corrupt, and never before visited. She asked the woman's forgiveness on behalf of her husband, and begged her to desist from a course that would bring injury to Khiradasundari's husband and family. The woman paid no heed to this plea. She continued to lie still, shrouded in silence and pain, and undeterred. After three days and three nights in the mansion, the woman died.

It was said that when she was so close to death that

some watchers thought she had actually passed on, she parted her cracked and bleeding lips to speak. The last words of her life echoed those she had said to Pratap Narayan three days ago—'if I have been a good woman in my life, this house will fall under my curse. Nothing will survive.'

Seven days after she died, Pratap Narayan returned home. He had been bitten by a snake beside the road, and had died shortly after the bite. He came back on a bier.

Pratap Narayan's son, Surya Narayan, inherited the family's considerable estate at quite a young age. Like his father, he was not particularly far-sighted. Also like his father, he was happy to spend. Unlike his father however, he did not covet the wives of other men, but had his own addictions. His was a deep attraction to renowned female performers, the irresistible women of skill called baijis, and he brought them in from everywhere—Lucknow, Delhi, Agra, Benaras, Lahore, Calcutta. He squandered with both hands the fortune his father and grandfather had built, dedicating his life to the pursuit of music and the entertainment provided by beautiful women.

In deference to the wishes of the family, Surya Narayan married young. In another departure from his father's temperament, he did not despise his wife. He did, however, almost entirely avoid her. Occasionally very late at night, drunk and sated with entertainment, he would weave his way to his wife's rooms in the inner quarters. These moments were exceedingly rare. It was well known in Palashpur that most of his adult life was spent in the outer chambers of the mansion, where his beloveds of the moment were usually located.

His other passion was travel. Surya Narayan travelled extensively, but the manner of his travel bore a peculiar quirk. He had visited numerous sites of pilgrimage but had never actually completed the journey by standing in front of the deity and asking for blessings. Once close to the outer walls of a temple that he had started out to see, he would turn around and return without entering the inner sanctum. When questioned about this strange caprice, he would say wryly, 'I've been a sinner most of my life. Why would I defile a sacred space by entering it?'

Surya Narayan died relatively young and quite suddenly, of cholera. The enormous debt he left behind was fully calculated only after he was gone, and the burden to carry it fell on his still-juvenile son, Shankarnarayan.

By the time Shankarnarayan came of age, the house was all that was left of the Choudhury fortune. Every source that had over the last two generations fed the family fortune, was dried up, or had been spent or gambled away. No one in the family was able to go out and earn a living, since years of access to unlimited resources had rendered them utterly incapable of fending for themselves. The little jewellery that was still left in the house was sold to raise Shankarnarayan.

He turned out to be very different from his father and grandfather. Indifferent towards the British and their ways, he turned instead towards religion, the study of Sanskrit, and an overdeveloped reverence for social rituals and mores. He was an unsmiling, conservative, religious man, obsessively devoted to the particular avatar of Lakshmi the family considered their goddess of fortune and protection. Shankarnarayan did not talk much, always ate at home, and was almost certain to be found at any time in his room on the third floor of the house. While still quite young, he dressed in saffron robes and prayer beads, shaved his head, and virtually became a hermit.

Playing violin was Shankarnarayan's only vice. He loved to play the violin, but unfortunately was not particularly good at it. When he sat sawing wildly at his violin at night, the sounds that came from the instrument sounded less like music, and more like a woman's voice shrieking in pain, loss and fear. The wailing would echo around the grounds, and superstitious people would whisper among themselves that it sounded as if the goddess of the house was being tortured in the third floor room where the master played.

Family tradition dictated that Shankarnarayan should marry, and so he did. His son was born some years after. He broke with family tradition in that he did not dislike his wife, Kalyani, but felt no special affection for her either. She was a responsibility, a duty he had to perform, and so he did. However tenuous his marital relationship, this did not mean that he spent time outside. In fact no one had ever seen Shankarnarayan leave the house. His days were consumed by meditation and rituals to appease the family goddess. The worship would start early in the morning while it was still dark, and continue through the entire day. After a day spent in a variety of ceremonial rites and prayer, he would eat very sparingly and then retire to the third-floor room that he had inherited from his father.

He became a physical mirror of the Choudhury family's decline. As they fell to poverty, he too got thinner and thinner until he was skeletal. Driven almost mad by obsessive religiosity, he would sit hunched and muttering over his prayers, with only one desire, a sole objective for all the offerings to the goddess. 'Give me land,' he would pray, 'give me money, give me wealth, give me back everything my family lost.' He begged, prayed, cajoled, bribed and begged again, all day, and every day, but it never seemed to make a difference to the fortunes of the Choudhurys.

One moonless night in early spring, Shankarnarayan had a vivid dream. In the dream, he saw that the family goddess, upon whom he had lavished so much worship and devotion, was preparing to walk out of the Choudhury house. She was beautiful beyond belief, and graceful, and surrounded by an ethereal light that somehow illuminated the whole world. In his dream, he got up and ran to block the goddess's path. She looked at him with sadness on her face—'Child, why are you blocking my path? Let me go.'

Crushed by her words, Shankarnarayan cried out, ‘Mother, how can you leave us like this?’

She laughed aloud, and wanton cruelty blossomed on that impossibly beautiful face. Too caught up in his own fear of loss to notice the transformation, he persisted desperately, ‘I have so often gone without food so that everything I have may be poured into the worship of your glory! Is this not enough? What more do you want?’

‘No, this is not enough,’ said the goddess, ‘I want blood.’

‘Whose blood do you want, my lady?’

‘I want your son’s blood.’

The goddess vanished, and Shankarnarayan woke up with a start. He was trembling, and sweating all over as if it was humid mid-summer. He sat on his bed and wept and shivered. What kind of test of devotion was this? Only a monster could set him such a test! And yet, the fragrance of lotus that had surrounded the goddess in his dream still lingered in the room, he could smell it clearly. There was no doubt that the goddess had actually come to see him. Shankarnarayan felt his doubts melt away, and his objective become fixed. He would give the goddess what she wanted. No matter what the cost, the goddess must not be allowed to leave.

He walked quietly through the dark, still house, to his wife’s bedroom. Kalyani was lying on her bed with their young son by her side, both deeply asleep. His son was no longer an infant, but still quite young, and light enough to be picked up and removed from his mother's side with ease. Shankarnarayan took the boy carefully from his wife's side, and holding him close, quietly left the room. Kalyani stirred and turned, but did not open her eyes.

He retraced his steps through the house, carrying the boy very carefully so he would not wake. When he stepped out of the inner quarters of the building, a high, sharp wind was blowing hard, whistling through the treetops and heralding a rising storm. He held the boy closer, and the child, comfortable against his father's chest, slept on. Shankarnarayan entered the temple of the family goddess, laid the boy gently down in front of the statue, and beheaded him.

Maybe the child cried out once, but the howling wind would have swept that sound away before anyone in that vast house could hear it. All that was left of the life of the child was blood, splattered blood all over the inner sanctum of the goddess's temple, much more blood than anyone would think a small child could contain. It seemed as if the entire temple had become stained with blood.

A man of less conviction than Shankarnarayan may have felt fear, or guilt, but driven as he was by deep inner belief, Shankarnarayan was not disconcerted. He viewed the blood as an inconvenience, something that needed to be cleaned up in order to restore to neatness the place of the goddess.

A quantity of sand had been stored in one side of the

outer sanctum. It was intended to line the floor under the ritual fire he frequently built for prayer. He fetched this sand, and started to use it to try and clean up the blood. At some point during this effort to clean—perhaps just before daybreak, Shankarnarayan fell asleep on the floor, surrounded by bloody sand.

Kalyani awoke with the sun, and discovered her boy was gone. She searched in the usual places of the inner quarters, but found no sign of him. It was then that she started to get alarmed. By the time she ran out of the residential part of the mansion, she was already screaming like a mad thing—'have you seen the boy? Where did the child go?'

Shankarnarayan found that he could not look at his wife, could not answer her desperate questions. He had thrown their child's body into the deepest part of the river, where the current was relentless. No one could possibly know where the child was now. All that was left of him was the bloody sand in the inner sanctum of the temple.

Sensing something was very wrong, Kalyani shouted at her husband, 'Say something! Please tell me where he is? No, you don't have to tell me, just bring back my son to me!' But he could not respond to her questions in any way.

The ugliness of the affair could not be hushed up. Kalyani was an intelligent woman, and she understood without being told that her untrustworthy, obsessive husband must have done something evil that had cost her her son. She retired to her bed in frozen and helpless silence. One night, not long after, she got up and walked to the river in which her husband had thrown the dead body of her beloved son, and drowned herself. Some days after this, Shankarnarayan Choudhury disappeared from the house. No one saw him leave, and he was never seen again.

But all this happened more than fifty years ago. No one knows if anyone still lives in some forgotten corner of the crumbling shell of the house. No one knows if the family goddess is still imprisoned in the family temple, since her hunger was sated all those years ago. All that is left are rumours that on some nights of wind and rain, any brave soul venturing close to the broken mansion may hear on the air a sound that is entirely out of place in such a ruin. It is a low, satisfied, happy laugh, almost a chuckle. It is the sort of merriment that one may suppress with a hand because the joy it expresses will be taken badly by others.

This rumour, and the laugh that some may hear, is all that remains of the Choudhury fortune.

The Ghosts of Spices

Moshla bhut

THE AFTERNOON WHOLESALE spice market at Burrabazar has just opened. Hazari Biswas and his large potbelly are settled comfortably at his shop in the market. It's still early for local buyers, so things are slow. Many of the current shoppers in the market look like they're from the suburbs, stocking up.

Hazari's shop is almost empty. He is fanning himself with a dried-leaf hand fan, and trying to keep awake. Sometimes he loses the battle with sleep, and his head droops noticeably forward. Suddenly, he hears a familiar voice calling his name, and it is loud enough to jerk him awake.

The loud voice belongs to his friend, Jatin Bhadra. Not content with pulling Hazari out of a pleasant, hazy semi-nap state, Jatin leans his walking stick at a corner, comes into the shop, and theatrically collapses on the four-legged stool in front of Hazari.

Jatin and Hazari are the same age, and good friends.

Fortune had not smiled on Jatin of late, until Hazari had a serious talk with him and advised that he become a middleman of spices. Now things are going better for Jatin because he is earning quite well at his new trade. In fact, Jatin is doing so well, that nowadays Hazari listens carefully to Jatin's plans and schemes in the world of wholesale spices. At least some of those plans have already made him more profit than he expected.

'Look, you can't make money by sitting in your shop and hoping that customers will come by,' Jatin sounded quite definite. 'That way you'll only fall asleep. It's very important that you watch and listen, and keep track of what's going on.'

'What's going on?' asked Hazari. 'It's good to see you, I hope you're doing well.'

Jatin ignored the formalities. 'That's exactly why I've come to see you. It's not easy to get this information, I had to talk to many contacts, do a lot of legwork. I come to you because you know that Jatin Bhadra tends to talk too much, but the information he brings is always sound. Ok, now the real news. Listen carefully.'

Jatin dragged his stool closer to Hazari and indicated that they should keep their voices down. Hazari could almost smell the possibility of money in this surreptitious behaviour, so he leaned closer, and prepared to pay more attention than he ever paid to any religious or spiritual reading.

Apparently, a large Graham Trading Company ship called the SS Rangoon had been loaded to capacity with valuable goods somewhere in the Dutch East Indies. It was headed to the Calcutta Port to offload its cargo, which consisted mainly of numerous sacks of expensive spices—dried chilies, turmeric, cumin and bay leaves among them. It was rumoured that these sacks were no less than eighty to a hundred kilos each, and that the ship was crammed from bow to stern with these high-value sacks.

There was dense fog the night this loaded ship turned into the Ganga, on the last leg of its trip to Calcutta. The pilot of the ship was used to high seas, not the narrow delta straits at the mouth of the river. He got confused in the fog, and ended up grounding the ship quite badly in the seasonal shallows. The ship was loaded, sitting heavy and low in the water. This episode did real damage. The now badly hurt ship continued limping upstream, hoping to get near enough to Calcutta port to be rescued, but did not make it. It sank near Diamond Harbour, taking its merchandise, and many of its sailors.

Most of the valuable merchandise went under. Some of it, though, did not sink with the ship. The sacks that did not sink, which were mainly of dry spices, were found floating in the midstream current of the river. They had been hooked or otherwise dragged to shore by the Port Authorities. It was being whispered around that the spices in those sacks floated because they had been packed very well, so well that the water had not been able to damage them at all. Those sacks were due to be auctioned off by the Port Commissioner's office at eight the next morning.

The business-minded Hazari Biswas immediately understood the importance of the information his friend had brought. He had after all made quite a fortune by cheating and out-manoeuvring other people, and quickly acting on any inside information that he had ever been privy to. Plans were immediately made between the two.

Before he left, Jatin made sure to reinforce the significance of the opportunity he had brought to Hazari. 'Remember, brother, if you want to make money, do not let such a chance at fortune pass you by! They just want to get rid of the goods, so the prices will be very low. The actual auction will start at eight thirty, but I will meet you at seven to be on the safe side, and we will go on from there.'

The next morning, as planned, Hazari and Jatin went to the Khidirpur docks. They could hear the loud confusion around the venue of the auction from quite a distance. Evidently, more people had got wind of this opportunity than they had thought. Jatin had been walking faster, in front, and Hazari slower, behind. When they came within view of the venue, Hazari suddenly speeded up to a fast trot. Ignoring all the other many people in the enormous warehouse, he headed straight for the white man who represented the Port Commissioner. He and the man whispered back and forth for a bit, then Hazari ran to the auction table and stopped the auction from opening for bids.

'What happened there?' said Jatin. 'I hope you've been able to fix it properly, no loose ends?'

Hazari looked brisk and businesslike 'It's done. I'll tell you in detail, later. Did you count the sacks in the lot? How many sacks do they have?'

'They have about a hundred sacks.'

A hundred sacks of expensive spices! There they were, piled almost to the roof, looking to Hazari's greedy eyes like classical columns in some vast, wealthy hall. Who could imagine that such dazzling fortune would favour him, Hazari Biswas, of all people! Now there was just one task left, and it would be a difficult one. The sacks would have to be safely moved from the Port Commission to Hazari's storage and somehow fitted into that limited space. He could heave a deep sigh of relief once that was done, not before.

'Let's not delay completing this auspicious task,' Hazari beamed at Jatin. 'You arrange the transport for the goods, and I'll go ahead to ensure that everything is ready for the sacks to arrive at my storage.' He hurried away, leaving Jatin to deal with the logistics.

All the sacks did not fit at once in the hired vehicle, which had to come back to make another loaded trip. It was late in the afternoon by the time Jatin, with the second load, arrived at the storage area attached to Hazari's shop.

It was immediately evident that no successful plans had been made to accommodate the valuable merchandise. The sacks that had been delivered in the earlier lot were lying around on the dusty pavement outside the shop. Hazari had hired only three men to move them in. In the absence of proper directions, these men were milling around, doing nothing. A large crowd of curious onlookers had gathered, and they were getting perilously close to the unguarded sacks. Hazari himself was present, but largely useless, since all he seemed to be doing was yelling at various people. The police, also present, were getting annoyed. They wanted the sacks off the public pavement as soon as possible.

Jatin felt that some organization was urgently required, so he entered the fray. What followed was an evening of very hard work. But by the time darkness fell, all the sacks were off the pavement and had somehow been bundled into Hazari's godown. They had been crammed in, and stacked one on top of the other until they were pressing against the roof, but they were in and safe. Rearranging them to fit without damage to the valuable contents took some more hours, so it was about ten o'clock by the time Jatin and Hazari were able to return home that night. The last thing they did was to securely lock the main door of the godown, and leave an employee of Hazari's sleeping, in a way that he blocked the door, as he did every night.

It was much later at night, late enough to be almost very early morning. Other men who slept in the market, guarding other godowns for their employers, were woken up by sounds that seemed to be coming from inside Hazari's godown. Given the events of the previous day, they suspected theft. One of them woke Hazari's guard, who was sleeping at his place in front of the doors of the godown. He woke up and searched as thoroughly as he could, but there was no sign of any illegal entrance to the godown. The front door, before which he slept, was still securely locked, and the windows were firmly shut and bolted from the inside. Being a long-term employee at this business, he knew that there were no other entrance and exit points to the room. Yet, it was undeniable that sounds, including occasional quite loud banging and shoving sounds, were coming from inside the room. All the other wide-eyed men in the market could hear them clearly, and it was just as clear that they were coming from Hazari's godown. There was no possibility of error with the direction of the noises. The guard had not been left with a key, so he could not open the room to check inside. He waited helplessly at his appointed spot outside the door as the inexplicable noises went on. They finally became softer as day broke, and over the next half-hour or so, they stopped entirely.

Rumours flew like wildfire around the spice market in the morning. Hazari's godown had been broken into! Everything was gone! The popular assumption was that the thieves must have made a clean sweep, because the noises had been so loud, and gone on for a long time. As with rumours of such spectacular nature, these rumours spread fast. Hazari woke up at home to hear that his recently-acquired riches had disappeared overnight.

He came running to the spice market with his heart

in his mouth, and unlocked the godown. Nothing had been disturbed inside. All the sacks were waiting quietly in the same way they had been stacked the evening before. Torn between relief and anger, Hazari concluded that this was the work of mischief-mongers and spreaders of rumour. His competition at the market had seen the sacks of spices the evening before, they must have been driven by jealousy to make trouble.

But then, what of the report of the trusted guard on his payroll? Horay had heard the sounds too, frighteningly loud and clear he said. Thieves were the only explanation, but how could one thief, let alone several, enter a room so securely closed up? And why would they make such a ruckus that the entire market became aware that they were at work? Was someone trying to scare him? But why? Hazari was baffled. It just made no sense at all. He decided that the time for delegation was over. He would stay overnight at the spice market and guard the godown himself.

Hazari and Horay spent that evening checking the godown from corner to corner. They climbed over, and poked between the sacks to ensure that they had examined every inch of wall, ceiling and floor—but no gap or break was found. As evening fell, Hazari opened the single barred window of the godown so he would be able to look in, left the room, and locked the main door behind him. Taking no chances, he used two four-lever padlocks. Then Horay and he settled down in front of the door, at the spot Horay usually slept alone. They talked and dozed lightly with ears open for any untoward sound or movement, but all was calm. It was almost two in the morning when they both finally fell asleep.

Hazari woke up with a start a few hours later. He had heard a sound from inside the godown. Horay had already heard sounds, but he had clear memories of the night before and decided it would be safer to let his boss lead the charge. He was lying quietly with his eyes shut, giving no sign that he was anything but sound asleep.

But what were those strange noises from inside? Muffled dragging and shuffling sounds had woken both the men up, these were sounds that were possible to miss unless part of the mind was listening for them. As they woke, however, the sounds got louder. It felt like things were being shoved carelessly around, pushed and pulled. Things were being struck and banged and thrown with no regard for any listeners. Strangest of all, it felt like someone, or more than one fist, was banging on the door from the inside, trying to get out.

It was impossible to lie still in the face of such an onslaught. Hazari and Horay got up in a stumble and checked the two heavy locks on the door. The locks, and the door on which they hung were utterly undisturbed, even as furious thumping sounds went on from the other side. Shaking, Hazari crept to the open window and peered into the godown. It was dark in the room, but it seemed to him that he could just make out the shadows of two of the larger sacks, which now appeared to be placed against the door, on the inside. It seemed to him that these sacks were banging repeatedly against the door.

Hazari felt a rapid descent into fear, tinged with confusion. Had the sacks come alive then? Was his mind going, taking his eyesight with it? Was he hallucinating from dread and the lack of sleep? Finding himself completely unable to cope, he took the path of least resistance and fell back from the window. Then he squeezed his eyes shut and decided to refuse to open them for any reason. If he couldn't see it, it couldn't hurt him.

He must have fallen asleep, because when he awoke it was daylight. Early sunlight was streaming into the godown through the bars on the window. There were no more noises coming from inside the room. Horay, who was already awake—or had not slept at all—commented that this was exactly like the day before, when, too, the strange sounds had disappeared with the daylight.

Hazari quickly went to the door and unlocked both padlocks. The door was clear as he stepped in, noting the lack of large sacks crowding the door on the inside. Everything was as he had left it—but, wait a moment! Nothing appeared to be missing, but everything was not as it had been last evening. The sacks appeared to have been shifted, they were no longer occupying the spots at which they had been originally stashed. It was as if someone had broken into the godown and spent the night shifting each sack away from its old position, to a new one. Some of this disturbance was subtle, a few inches to the left or right, sacks leaning differently in their new positions, but some, as with the four or five big sacks at the back, the difference was patently obvious. There could be no mistake about those big sacks. They had definitely been roughly moved.

Hazari was gobsmacked. These were strange thieves indeed. To take the trouble to break into a godown with no visible entrances, move the valuable contents around loudly and at random, and then leave with no goods? What kind of thieves behaved in this irrational way? If not thieves, then what? Ghosts? The ghosts of those who drowned with the ship? Finding himself on truly slippery territory, Hazari gave up. The only thing to do was to guard the spices, nothing else mattered.

It had been just two nights since he had bought goods from the shipwreck. Hazari was now crazed with unspecified suspicion. He hired three strong men to stand guard with him through the third night. He left his shop and went home to sleep all day so he could be completely awake through the night. That night, Hazari and the three men took their places outside the securely locked door to the godown. He was determined. This was the night that he would be avenged on the miscreants who had deliberately messed with his peace of mind. Once he got his hands on even one of them—well, that was what the hired strongmen were for. He sat awake while time crept by. There was silence, apart from the clock in the next establishment striking the hours.

It was four in the morning. The sound of the fourth

strike of the gong was still reverberating its last clear bass when Hazari heard a parallel sound, one that made him straighten up and stare incredulously at the locked door. From inside the room came the sound of many people drawing breath, and exhaling, together. There was a long, hard, indrawn breath, followed by a long, strong exhalation. The exhale was so distinct and loud that it sounded like enough wind was being pushed out to start a storm.

Hazari immediately awoke the men he had hired. He told two of them to run and check the back of the building, because he was sure the breathing thieves had cut a passage in from there. Once they had run off to check the back, he turned his attention to the main door, which was still locked.

He unlocked the door and threw it open, confident that this would be the night he would catch the troublemakers who had been playing havoc with his property and his mind. But there were no thieves inside. There was also no sign of a break in the wall. The room, however, was not empty. It was full of a large number of very impatient sacks. You could tell they were impatient from the way they were hopping up and down, breaking into little jigs, and generally showing a disinclination to behave like the normal patient sacks of the everyday world.

The hired men took one look at this extravagantly unexpected sight, shivered with fear, and took off at speed. Hazari was left alone to deal with anything that would follow.

What followed was a kind of march-past, to which Hazari was the gaping onlooker. One by one, the sacks marched out of the godown and onto the road outside. Once there, they milled about uncertainly, as if they were confused about what to do next. Suddenly, it seemed as if a large sack of very expensive salt decided that it had had enough of this indecision. It set off at a canter down the road. To Hazari's horror, the other sacks followed. They were very disciplined, for sacks. A single file of sacks of all kinds of valuable spices—the first part of the line made of the goods that Hazari had cheated out of auction, and the second part made of sacks that had already been occupying the godown when the windfall was moved in, three days ago. Making the rear of this remarkable procession was the man who was following a large portion of his earthly belongings down the street.

The procession marched briskly down Strand Road. It appeared to be following the tramlines set into the ground. At the far end of Strand Road, it turned left towards the river.

Day lightened the sky over the enormous river. Fluffy clouds drifted by on a slight breeze. The surface of the water became slowly more visible under the glow of the dawn sky. Hazari Biswas stood alone on an embankment beside the river with the air of a man not quite in command of the facts. He was cocooned in a sense of total disbelief. Passers-by called to him to get off the embankment, but he did not hear them. Was this a dream? No, this was no dream, this was a nightmare.

He watched as the sacks marched up to the river in the same determined and disciplined fashion that they had adopted to get there. Once at the brink of the fast-flowing water, the sacks threw themselves, one by one, into the river. As with the procession, the spices acquired from the shipwreck went first, and Hazari's older stock went later. But they all went into the Ganga, and the current bore them rapidly away. Hazari Biswas's business was decimated, overnight.

Such news spreads fast. When it reached back to the spice market, the shopkeepers of neighbouring shops were not sympathetic. They shook their heads in a knowing way. Some were heard to say that they were not surprised at how it had turned out, and thank goodness that they had not been tempted into buying haunted goods themselves.

'A ship is wrecked on a night of new moon, not a sliver of light on the river,' a shopkeeper was heard to say, 'it goes down with much of its crew, they drown with the vessel, death so far from home. And then, stingy Hazari Biswas goes and buys all of the shipwrecked goods, for cheap. What did he really expect was going to happen?'

Arrack

Arrack

When I worked at the Lahore Museum, I was fortunate to befriend the well-known newspaperman and publisher Vinayak Dutt Singh. Mr Dutt Singh's family was an old one, but it was not originally from Lahore in the Punjab, it was from Kota in Rajasthan. His family had moved to Lahore for work only three generations ago. Before that, they were royalty in Rajasthan.

Once the hot days cooled off towards the evening, I would walk over to his house. We usually sat in the living room, surrounded by the trappings of the Rajasthani royal history of his family—armour, flags, clubs, swords and various other items of warlike persuasion were tastefully displayed in the room. I very much enjoyed discussing both history and current affairs with his unique perspective, surrounded by all these memorabilia of a not-too-distant, and evidently thoroughly colourful past. These evenings were particularly interesting when Mr Dutt Singh felt minded to talk about the history of

Rajasthan, and specially about the Kota area, in which he was widely considered an expert.

One winter evening, I reached his house after dusk and went straight to the living room, as was my habit. It was very cold. Two cups of hot tea and several smokes later I was feeling quite revived and ready to spend the evening in pleasant conversation, when suddenly—and I don't quite know why—I asked him, 'Tell me, Mr Singh, do you believe in the supernatural?'

He gave my question some thought. Then he said, 'Yes, I do.'

'Have you ever seen ghosts, or anything like that?'

Again, the quiet consideration. 'That is not my story,' he said. 'It is my grand-uncle's story. But if those events had not occurred in my family, we would have still been very large landholders in Rajasthan, receiving the kind of respect given to royal lineage. We would not have had to move to Lahore, and all these years later, I would not have to work for a living. It was a very strange event that led to all this.'

'What kind of event was this?' I asked, my curiosity thoroughly roused.

'Listen, then. The man I called my younger grandfather was not my grandfather's own brother, but they were closely related by marriage. I always thought of him as my other grandfather. When he was young, he was a man who went in active pursuit of the good things in life. He was also very handsome.'

I looked at the tall, strong, aristocratic man in front

of me, and did not find it difficult to believe that other members of his family would be similarly blessed.

Mr Singh went on, 'I was very young when I saw him. Of course, by that time he was utterly insane.'

'Utterly insane?' I echoed, somewhat confused at the line this story was taking.

'Totally,' said Mr Singh. 'And this story is about how he went mad. When he lost his sanity, he also lost my family all our land, wealth and social standing, because those were the royal laws of Kota at the time. But anyway, that is another story. Let me tell you the real story, the one I started to tell.'

***

'There was an informal gathering place for soldiers from the Kota military a short distance from the village in which I was born. My other grandfather, who I simply called grandfather, would attend those gatherings from time to time, mostly for the arrack that was available there. He had some friends there too, they would drink together. One such drunken full-moon night, they decided they wanted to go swimming in the Ravi by the light of the moon. So they saddled up and rode for the river.

The mighty river Ravi flows leisurely through the desert in three tributaries. At the time of which I am talking, the first of these three stream-beds was completely dry. The middle stream had about knee-high water, that you could easily ride or wade through. After this, there was a wide open stretch of dry river-bed, through which ran the third, and largest of the streams. This was the only one of the tributaries which was full of running water like an actual river, and this is the one my grandfather and his friends headed to that night.

They reached the area and started to cross the dry parts of the river bed. Near the place the first tributary would flow when the river was in spate, one of my grandfather's drunken companions decided to get off his horse and lie down flat on the sand. His friends tried to encourage him to get up and come swimming with them, but he refused to move. So the other two people on the night's expedition—of which one was my grandfather—decided to let him do as he chose, and went on ahead toward the water. I am sure it is needless for me to emphasize how very inebriated all three of them were.

Two men were now riding towards the river. At a point they were already quite close to the water, my grandfather realised to his annoyance that his companion had stopped. Reining his horse in and turning to ask why, he saw that the man was looking fixedly at a far point on the rocky dunes of the river bed. There was both curiosity and fear on his face.

"What are you staring at?" demanded my grandfather.

His friend pointed at the direction towards which his attention had been drawn, and held a finger to his lips in the universal gesture that asks for silence. So far away on the riverbank that they looked indistinct even in the dazzling full moon, were a number of human figures. A little more concentration, and my grandfather saw that the figures appeared to be moving around, but in a restricted area. After watching for a while, he realised that the figures were actually holding hands and dancing in a circle.

Who could possibly be so joyful in the middle of the night that they would have to leave their homes and come to dance in such a desolate spot? Both the men were astonished at this inexplicable behaviour on the part of not one or two, but what looked like a group of people. Neither my grandfather nor his friend suggested going any closer to the group. I don't know why they didn't investigate this strange sight, because no one told me that part of the story. Perhaps the two drunk men assumed that it was the arrack that was giving them unbidden visions, and that such hallucinations were better ignored. This is probably the reason they did not talk about this strange episode at home at that time.

Some years went by.

There was a large saltwater lake in the middle of the desert about three miles from a further point on the main water channel of the Ravi. It was called the Nahara Nipat, or Tiger Lake. This lake was surrounded on almost all sides by ranges of hills, with the further views on clear days being that of mountains. Some of these hills were a thousand feet high, or taller. The lake and surrounding areas were known places to mine salt, so businessmen at the Kota court would be periodically granted permission to send salt-acquiring expeditions to this part of the desert.

A few years after the event described earlier in this story, my grandfather decided that he would journey through the desert to this lake in order to shoot sand-duck. He had heard that sizeable flocks of sand-duck descend onto this lake late at night, and this struck him as ideal conditions for bagging game. Word was that the ducks would not come down to the water if they saw human beings in the vicinity, so he planned to reach the lake in time to build himself a makeshift shack of grasses and weeds, and sit hidden in it until the ducks landed on the water.

While arrangements for this hunting expedition were going on, a few older people of the village objected quite strongly to such a plan. None of these people gave any concrete reasons for these objections. They just said that it would not be a good idea for my grandfather—or anyone—to be on the shores of that lake through the night. It was apparently not a good place. Among these objectors was an older Bhil known simply as Bauji. In his younger days, he had been part of a regular caravan sent by the court of Kota to collect salt from the pans in this area and deposit it at a desert godown belonging to the court, which was about a mile from the lake. He claimed that he had seen the skies over the lake light up suddenly in the middle of the night, so bright that it looked like daylight. Even from a far distance, he had heard strange sounds from the water when the skies were so lit up. Absolutely nobody, he emphasized, should even consider spending the night alone at that lake. Bauji added that a shepherd had once unknowingly spent the night close to the spot, and was found the next day pacing around near the salt godown, which was the only habitation for many miles. He had lost his mind entirely. No one could ever again get any sense out of him or his many ramblings.

These stories did not work as they were intended. My grandfather was not the kind of man to heed such subtle warnings. He understood partying, hunting and drinking, and he was used to approaching all of this with a kind of fierce lopsided courage, along with large amounts of the inability to change his mind when it was fixated on an object. When such a man decides to do something, it does not behoove him to retreat from that position.

When Bauji realised that my grandfather was not going to listen to his advice, he settled for a pointer. "Remember that there is less danger on the nights the flocks of duck actually land on the lake."

Grandfather asked, "Danger of what, exactly? Tigers?"

"There may be more dangerous things in the world than tigers," replied the old Bhil. "I don't know what they are. I have heard many stories, but I don't know what those dangerous things may actually be."

"Come with me," offered my grandfather, "And I shall see that you are well rewarded."

Unpersuaded, the old Bhil shook his head. "Forgive me, sir, but I would not spend a night on the shore of that lake even for a full hundred rupees, or more. We are Bhil. We have no fear of tigers. I have myself hunted and killed many tigers with my arrows. But tell me, do you really not believe that there are more fearful things in the world than tigers?"

Needless to say, the expedition continued as planned. One problem was that the territory around the lake was not as familiar as my grandfather would have liked. This was because the lake was about forty miles through the desert, distant enough that only very good reasons could take people from our area that far out.

Grandfather first went through the desert to a Bhil village which was seven or eight miles from the lake. The next day, he left the village early and walked those miles. The larger part of this walk was through the hill territory that was part of the desert. In the last stretch, he left the rugged uplands and descended slowly to the valley in which the lake stood. The vast surface of salt water in the lake was glittering like diamonds in the late afternoon sun, and there was no one in any direction as far as the eye could see.

There was plenty of time before dark, so he took the time to wander around and leisurely gather all the long grasses, twigs, and creepers that he could. As evening lengthened the shadows, he used these to fashion a crude shelter that would keep him invisible to even quite low-flying ducks. Flocks of parrots in their last excursions before dark came in, and swooped down on the lake while he worked. But the solitude in the place continued to be absolute. Clearly, it was devoid of either human or animal life.

Even the last light on the faraway mountains had faded by the time the little shack was done. Grandfather then crept into it with his gun and some provisions he had carried from home, and settled to wait.

The full moon had passed two days ago so it was waning, but still bright over the open land. Once darkness fell entirely, the light of the moon gleamed and sparkled on the waters of the lake. The warmth of the day faded quickly, and it got colder as the night got deeper. The duck were expected to come to the water only after the mercury dropped. My grandfather waited for what felt like hours, but no sand-ducks arrived at the lake.

At the back of his mind he started thinking of what the old man had said—that the landing of the birds on the water meant that there was no danger on that night. What did the words mean, exactly? Did they imply that there was danger on the nights the ducks did not land? What kind of danger? Did tigers come down from the surrounding hills to drink water at the lake on the nights the ducks stayed away? Or did the ducks refuse to land on the nights tigers were due?

The night got deeper. Moonlight continued to glisten on the still waters of the lake. The dunes of the desert stood out in sharp relief, moonward sides lit bright, sides away from the moon wrapped in dark, mysterious shadow. There was absolute silence over the land and water. This scene of peace made my grandfather nervous, for reasons he did not understand. There was something eerie about this beauty, something that felt like it was slowly crawling under his skin. He took a few swigs of arrack from a leather flask and felt a little calmer. Then he pushed his unreasoning feelings aside and continued methodically scanning the unmoving vista in front of him, as a good hunter always does.

He was scanning the western side of the lake for the unnumbered time, when his eyes suddenly stopped as his heart leapt with joy. For there they were, a small flock of sand-duck, coming in to land at the water! How beautifully the moon shone on their snow-white wings!

The flock came in slowly, and settled on a sandy part of the shore very close to the water. The place they sat was across the water, quite far from my grandfather's shelter. It was close enough that his eyes were able to make out that the birds were on the ground, but distant enough to blur out any more detail than that. The moonlight, dazzling bright off the water and the sand, almost blinded him, making it difficult to keep a sense of visual perspective. He would certainly not be able to accurately aim his gun from the shelter.

Now that the target was in sight, all of my grandfather's apprehensions melted away. He was on firm ground here. All he needed to do was to wait, and inevitably, the birds would draw closer to his shelter and his gun. After all, the patience of a hunter is his most valuable asset. All he really needed to do now was not take his eyes off the ducks.

As his eyes adjusted though, the prickling fear he thought he had overcome returned in full strength. He knuckled his eyes as if to clear them of smoke, with the thought running clear and sharp through his mind—these are birds? What kinds of birds are these?

For as his eyes adjusted, he was able to see that the creatures that had landed on the shore were larger than birds—much, much larger. And they did not appear to be moving on land in the distinctive manner of ducks, or indeed any kind of bird. Then, the strangest idea filled his head. "Those are not birds at all," thought my grandfather in a kind of shock, "I think they could be human beings!"

I was probably looking extremely disbelieving, because Mr Singh stopped his narrative and addressed me directly. "I leave it entirely up to you, if you want to believe this or not," he said. "I heard this story many times from my grandfather, and from others too. It is an event in the history of my family. All I ask is that you do not think that I am making this up, or lying to you." My answering nod must have been convincing, because he continued.

'My poor grandfather wiped his eyes again, trying to clear them of whatever fog was clouding them. "But I took only a few sips of arrack," he thought, feeling somewhat pathetic. "How can that harm my mind and eyes like this?"

As this confusion rose to fill his thoughts, the creatures moved towards the water. They slid into the water and swam around, exactly like water-birds, and the swimming brought the flock towards the middle of the lake and closer to my grandfather. As the distance narrowed, it became absolutely clear that these were not birds of any kind. In fact, thought my utterly befuddled grandfather, they could be—women? With wings?

Yes, that is what the evidence of his eyes told him. They were beautiful women with flawlessly white wings, graceful like swans, frolicking on a lake in the middle of the desert two nights gone full moon.

He heard their happy laughter as they played and swam around, he heard the splashing of the water. No bird displaces so much water, he noted in a far recess of his mind. His eyes were spellbound by the grace and beauty of the swan-women, their laughter, their play. They seemed to have no idea that he was there and watching, or they did not care.

Grandfather had no idea how long he watched them before falling into a kind of swoon. He did remember coming to consciousness at one point, to see the shapes of swan-women silhouetted against the light sparkling off the water. They flapped their gorgeous white wings to rise from the lake, and then lazily rode the thermal currents until they disappeared into the eastern sky. An incredibly alluring wild scent still hung in the air. Unable to move, grandfather stayed huddled in the shack. His mind was divided between disbelief and fear, but there were also the beginnings of a strange desire.

The moon sank slowly in the sky and the night melted away into the very early dawn. Grandfather shook himself as the sky lightened, and crawled out of the shelter. Then, head still reeling, he started the walk back to the Bhil village from which he had come the day before.

Bauji was curious. "Did the duck land last night?" He asked, as soon as he saw the returning hunter.

"The duck came," my grandfather lied without missing a beat, "but I couldn't shoot even one." Grandfather was not accustomed to lying, but the old Bhil would certainly have forbidden the idea which was taking nascent shape in his mind.

An irresistible tug that would not be denied started in his mind early the next day. By evening, he was settled back in his makeshift shelter by the lake, gun and flask of arrack at the ready. The duck came that night, flocks of actual sand-duck, swooping and flapping over the lake, behaving exactly like the waterfowl they clearly were. Grandfather lay in his shack and watched them play on the water. He took an occasional swig of arrack, but could not find it in his heart to use the gun.

This routine went on for a number of nights. He would feel irresistibly compelled to walk to the lake and stay concealed all night, drinking and watching the sand-ducks on the water till dawn. Then, exhausted, he would return to the village and deep, dreamless sleep.

On the last of these nights, in the hour just before

dawn, my grandfather was settled in the shack and lazily scanning the horizon when his heart leaped again, exactly as it had so many nights before. There they were, the ethereally beautiful winged creatures, coming in to land at the lake! They were distinctly visible in the half-light. The previous episode had not been a hallucination, then. These swan-like beings were certainly not birds of any kind.

Trembling with excitement, he watched them slide gracefully into the water. This time they swam in a much wider area of the lake, separating out from each other, laughing and calling to each other in an unknown tongue, with moonlight sparkling off the water on their big, powerful wings. Some of the swimmers came quite close to where he sat entranced, his breathing reduced to shallow gasps. He saw how astonishingly beautiful, and yet somehow unreal those faces were, how elemental and how entirely free. Grandfather became suffocatingly wrapped in an all-encompassing desire to possess. He would have to have one of them, or he would never be able to breathe properly again.

Perhaps it was the arrack. Perhaps it was the days of pent-up excitement and repeated disappointment. Most likely it was a combination of the two, but at this point my grandfather did the stupidest thing he had ever done. He stumbled out of the shack and ran towards the creatures closest to him, the ones swimming at the shore directly in front of the shack. His befuddled, exhausted, misguided brain must have convinced him that he had a chance to catch and imprison one of those otherworldly women, to possess it entirely. In that insane moment, it must have felt like an opportunity that must not be missed.

There was a brief flash of alarmed faces, and a flurry of large wings shaking off water. Then, as smoothly and quickly as they had appeared, the swan women took flight and disappeared into the first pink of the eastern sky. It was like that—one instant they were flying away, and the next instant they were gone from sight, and the sky was clear.

Grandfather was found the next afternoon by a fisherman who had walked a long way to try his luck at the lake. The fisherman said that he had been talking loudly and incoherently to himself in great excitement, while gesticulating and pacing about near the water. It did not take a doctor to understand that his mental balance had been severely disturbed. The kind man took him by the hand and led him gently to the nearest village, which was the one at which he was based. Seeing my grandfather in this condition, Bauji shook his head sorrowfully. "I warned him that there was danger on the nights the ducks would not land," was all he said.

I remember my grandfather as a confused, unstable presence with obvious mental problems. But he would suddenly and unpredictably become quite coherent, and then he would tell us this story, not once, but several times. His periods of wellness became shorter as he grew older, and in the last ten years of his life nobody could understand anything he said. He died absolutely insane.'

***

'This is a really strange story,' I ventured. 'These events, they seem—'

'Difficult to believe in this century, I know,' said Mr Singh. 'But keep in mind that all this happened quite a long time ago, the world was different then. In any case, there are members of my family who don't believe a word of it. They say the man just drank too much arrack for his own good and hallucinated fairies out in the desert. And there are those, some not of my family, who say that when a man spends the night out in the desert and spies on fairies, he is never allowed to have a coherent mind again.'

Mr Singh smiled. 'I wouldn't know, either way. I wasn't even born then.'

The House of His Foremothers

Poitrik Bhima

THE BIG HOUSE was on the banks of the Madhumati.

Radhamohan sat on a balcony facing the river, a book in his hands. He was trying to read, but the loveliness of the surroundings had captured his gaze. It's such a beautiful property, he thought. The pretty little river, thickets of bamboo on both sides of the water. Behind the house, a mango orchard so overgrown with lush green that it looks like an ancient forest. He enjoyed having such a large house to himself. The quietness made it a perfect place to study or write, far away from the continuous noise of the city.

The house belonged to his family, but no one had lived there for a long time. No one had visited either, the house had been lying empty and hollow. Radhamohan's father had been born in this house, but his father—Radhamohan's grandfather—had moved the family out when his son was still a child. Radhamohan's grandmother came from Medinipur, and it was to her family home that her children were moved. Radhamohan's father completed school and law school in Medinipur, then went on to make a lot of money as a practising lawyer. He built a large house in Medinipur and lived there with his family.

It wasn't that Radhamohan's grandfather had entirely abandoned the ancestral home. He did visit, but sparingly, and he never stayed too long. Up to recently, the house had been maintained by distant relatives who lived in the village. However, a slowdown of economic activity in the area had made it difficult for those relatives to earn a living while continuing to live in the village. So they had been forced to move to the city, and Radhamohan's ancestral home was no longer maintained as the big old house needed to be.

Enough time had passed after the relative's departure for the grounds to be returning slowly to jungle. The house was also suffering from some quite serious disrepair. Action, comprising of either large-scale repair, or sale, would have to take place soon, or there would be a severe depreciation in the value of the property.

Radhamohan had completed his law degree the year before, and taken over his father's law practice. He was settling into a routine with work when a letter had come from the village, drawing his attention to the fact that the issue of the old house and property needed a resolution, preferably at the earliest. He waited for the break from work that the annual Pujas brought, and then travelled to deal with the question of the old house.

The neighbors here had been very kind. Bhairab, who was the closest neighbour had persuaded Radhamohan to have meals at his house, which was a few minutes' walk along a narrow path. The alternative was for Radhamohan to cook for himself, which he had been prepared to do. But it was obviously more convenient to eat at his neighbours, and he was very grateful for the hospitality.

Most of his neighbours had been delighted to see the big old house occupied again, if only by one young man. They wanted him to come home and have a meal with the family, and he had been moved by their genuine happiness at seeing him. He had accepted all the invitations that came his way. Now, he knew most of the families that lived nearby, and felt cocooned in their kindness.

Bhairab's older son brought him tea to the balcony. He sat and talked for a while, and then went back home. It was dusk by the time he left, and Radhamohan kept sitting on the balcony in the approaching darkness. The river began to reflect the clear, starry night sky as he sat sunk in thought. Why had his great-great-grandfather built this large house in such a distant place, with nothing else around? He was an inspector in the police. This was a respected position in those days, drawing a substantial salary. But he had no practical sense, apparently. Who builds a home for an entire family in a tiny village surrounded by jungle? How were the people living here supposed to earn a living? What kind of reason may have brought him to this remote location in the first place? Perhaps he could sell the whole thing off brick-by-brick—it was a big house, lots of well-made, good-quality brick—

There was a slight sound in the room behind him.

Radhamohan turned and saw that a girl, very fair, and maybe ten or eleven years old, was standing at the threshold of the balcony door and peeping out at him. There was a lit kerosene lantern in the room, and some of that light was spilling out onto the balcony. Neither he, nor the girl, were completely in the dark.

This must be Bhairab's youngest daughter. How kind of the man to send his children along to help Radhamohan. He called out, 'Hey little girl, have you come to tell me that dinner is ready?'

The girl went still as if startled, then she tentatively stepped out onto the balcony. 'What is your name?' asked Radhamohan.

'Lokkhi'

'That's a good name. Can you read?'

'Hm,' with a nod.

'Know any songs?'

'Hm,' another nod.

'That's very good,' said Radhamohan, laughing gently at the girl's sweet seriousness. 'Can you cook?'

'Hm,' a third, emphatic nod.

'That's a very important skill! What dishes can you cook?'

'Ev-ery-thing.'

'Everything! That's wonderful! You're a very talented little girl! Would you like to sit down?'

The girl shook her head as if she was embarrassed at being asked such a thing, 'No, I'm not going to sit.'

'Why not? Do you have work at home?'

'No.'

'Then sit?'

'No. I should go. You go and have dinner.'

'I'm going. Is dinner ready?'

'You must be hungry. Go and eat.'

Radhamohan turned away from her to get up and get ready for dinner. When he turned back towards her, she was gone. She must have run home.

Radhamohan proceeded towards dinner at a more leisurely pace.

After dinner, he walked back lost in thought about the house. He quite liked being alone there. He did not feel alone. It was as if the silent presence of his ancestors who continued to inhabit the house could see him, and regarded his presence with benevolent goodwill. His grandfather had played in this house as a child. His beloved grandmother had entered it as a hopeful new bride, pretty red-dye stained feet stepping over the threshold of the main door. They eventually made a life elsewhere and forgot this place, but it was as if the place did not forget them. That night, his ancestors came to him in dream. 'Why did you go away and forget us?' they asked with sorrow. 'What did we do to deserve this?'

The next day was spent out and about, dealing with the further reaches of the property. It was dark by the time Radhamohan had the time to go and sit in his favourite spot on the balcony. At first, he didn't realise that she was already there. A very quiet girl indeed, he thought once he saw her, how softly she walked to come and stand before him!

'Hey, little girl,' he said.

'Um.'

'Is dinner ready?'

'It'll be later, today. They're cooking mutton for you.'

'Oh, really? Today's a day of feasting, then!'

The girl smiled sweetly but said nothing. She's such a calm, agreeable presence, reflected Radhamohan. He was beginning to enjoy her peaceful company. 'Where are your mother's people from?' He asked, on impulse.

'I don't remember.'

'How can you forget? Don't you visit them?'

'No.'

Radhamohan felt a moment of deep appreciation for her fearless honesty.

'Why did you come alone?' She said, 'Bring your wife, bring your family. It's such a big house, you should all enjoy it.'

'Is that what you want, little girl?'

'Ve-ry mu-ch. That's what I want.'

'Why do you want that?'

'This huge house has been lying empty for so long. No one even lights a lamp in the evenings.'

Radhamohan was astonished at this kind of grown-up talk from a child. She must spend a lot of time with the older women of her family, who would be likely to have opinions like this.

'Do you feel bad that the lamps are not lit when it gets dark, little girl?' he asked gently. Perhaps she was scared by the big empty house so close to her own.

'Of course I feel bad! I want all of you to come here. I want the conches to be blown at dusk, and the lamps to be lit.'

She suddenly remembered something, and changed the topic. 'You must be very hungry. It's quite late now, and you haven't eaten.'

'No, no, not at all. It's not that late at all.'

'But you're used to having dinner early!'

'How do you know that I like having dinner early?'

She giggled with the mischief of a child, but said nothing.

They were both quiet for long enough for him to fall into a kind of reverie while gazing towards the river. The girl broke the silence.

'I really, really like it.'

Radhamohan looked at her. 'What do you like so much?'

'That you're here. Nobody comes here anymore.' She stopped for a moment, and then said briskly, 'Now you'd better get up and start walking, dinner is ready.'

'Really? How do you know that dinner is ready?'

She laughed, 'I just know,' she said. 'Go for dinner now.'

He got up from the chair and moved into the house, 'Just wait a minute?' he said 'I'll get ready, and we can walk to your house together.'

He did only take about a minute to freshen up, but when he returned, she was gone. She must have run ahead, because there was no sign of her on the path between the two houses. That's a sweet child, thought Radhamohan, while he walked the path. It's so funny how she talks like a grown little woman.

His neighbor was delighted to see him. 'Here you are! I was just about to send for you—dinner's finally ready. I'm so sorry that it's late today, cooking the meat took a long time. I thought you'd eaten our everyday humdrum home food for long enough. It was time for something special. After all, it's not every day that you will eat at our home—'

Radhamohan found himself embarrassed at this kindness, in a household that would need to stretch to provide this extra treat for him. But he ate well, and his neighbours were clearly so happy to feed him that he returned home satiated and happy.

The next evening, the girl came to visit him again. He was on his favourite chair on the balcony, listening to the river when he noticed her come in. 'Hey, little girl,' he said, 'I was just thinking of you.'

She smiled broadly, 'You were thinking of me?'

'Yes, I was, truly.'

She looked complacent. 'I know why you were thinking of me.'

'So tell me, why?'

'I know, but I won't tell you.'

Earlier that day, Radhamohan had got a box of locally famous sweets for her. Busy with other work, he had not gone to the market himself. Instead, he had asked Amulya, a manservant at the Nandi's, to run this errand for him. Hearing the girl's knowing tone, Radhamohan became convinced that Amulya had gossiped. It appeared that she already knew about the sweets that were intended to be a surprise. He had looked forward all day to her sudden joy when he put the box in her hands. Disappointed, he felt a fleeting but sharp irritation for the blabbermouth Amulya. Was nothing confidential in this village?

A peremptory voice arrested his uncharitable thoughts. 'Give me my sweets! Where are they?'

Radhamohan hurried into the house to get her sweets. When he came back to the balcony with them, the girl was gone. She's such a child, he thought. She's easily distracted, goes where her fancy takes her one moment to the next. He put the sweets away for the time being.

Radhamohan took the box with him when he went to the neighbours for dinner. 'She's such a shy child, she ran away before I could give this to her,' he said, handing the box to Bhairab.

Bhairab smiled genially, 'Oh, did our little girl visit you?'

'She comes to see me every day. We talk of this and that. I enjoy it very much.'

'I see, really? Well, yes, she is shy. I'm hoping it will pass as she grows older. After all, she's still quite young.'

The next day, as per the new routine, the girl came to his balcony in the evening. 'Where did you go yesterday?' asked Radhamohan 'I wanted to give you the sweets, but you ran away. I must say, I'm not happy with you for going away like that!'

The girl giggled at his clearly faked annoyance, but didn't say anything.

'Did you eat the sweets?' he asked her

'I didn't need to eat them. When you said that you had thought of me, and got them for me, that was enough.' She turned thoughtful for a moment. Then, in a tone of affection, she said, 'I like it so much, that you're here. The lamps are lit in the house every evening. I don't like it alone in the dark.'

'Come to the city with me?' offered Radhamohan

'All that is not for me. I'm all right here.'

'But it's the city! So many different things going on, so many lovely pictures, such a lot of wonderful things to eat!'

'Who cares about those things? Not me! You promise me that you'll come again!'

'I'll definitely come again, I like it here.'

'You didn't come all this time. The house was dark, nobody lit even one lamp at dusk! Well, anyway, I should go now. You're not leaving till Tuesday.'

Radhamohan was astonished. He did not recall telling Bhairab that he was planning to leave on Tuesday. But he must have mentioned it over dinner, and Bhairab must have passed it on to his family. How else would the girl know?

Radhamohan travelled in the surrounding villages over the next two days, completing the sundry administrative tasks that needed looking into before his return to Kolkata. Work done to his satisfaction, he returned to the big house on the river late on Monday night. It was too late to meet anyone from Bhairab's, or anyone else's family in the village. He had some dry snacks in a jar, so he made a dinner of that and went to sleep.

The next morning he was up and packing to leave, when Bhairab showed up, concerned. 'Where did you eat last night?' he asked, 'Why didn't you wake us up? There's always some food in the house. I hate to think that you went to sleep hungry!'

Radhamohan said, 'Will you please call your little girl? I'd really like to say goodbye to her before I leave.'

'Yes, yes, certainly, I'll just go and get her,' and Bhairab hurried homewards. He returned shortly thereafter, leading a pretty, wheaten complexioned girl, who looked about seven or eight years old. 'Not this girl,' said Radhamohan, 'her older sister'

'Her older sister?' Bhairab looked puzzled. 'Her older sister was married last year, she lives with her in-laws now. You've never met her older sister.'

'Then some other young girl of your family—'

'There are no other young girls in my family. She must be from some other part of the village—But no,

I don't know of any other girls in the village about this age. There's only a few families around here anyway.'

'She said her name was Lokkhi,' said Radhamohan, recalling their first conversation.

'Lokkhi? That's strange. There's nobody called Lokkhi in this village at all, of any age. You must have heard it wrong.' Radhamohan was willing to concede that he had heard the name wrong, but what about the little girl, his friend? Where had she come from? He couldn't possibly be mistaken about all the time they had spent together! So then, where had she gone? Or could it be that he was imagining the whole thing, his mind playing all kinds of detailed tricks on him? What an uncomfortable thought! He was troubled on the journey back, but his return to the city, his family, and all the work that had piled up during his absence quickly took over. He slowly forgot about the girl on the balcony.

Two years after this event, Radhamohan visited his aunt, his father's sister, in Jabalpur. He was leafing in a desultory manner through old family photo albums, when a face that seemed familiar caught his eye. He stopped, and tried to recall where and when he may have met someone who looked like that. Nothing came to mind.

He called his aunt and asked her where he may have met the girl in the picture. 'No, it's impossible, you've never met her,' she said. 'How could you have? This is my sister, your younger aunt. She died at the age of twelve. You were born a long time after she died. In fact your mother wasn't even married at that time. We used to live in the village house, beside that pretty river.'

His aunt continued, almost to herself, 'I remember so little about her, it was such a long time ago. After she died, our father did not want to live in that house anymore. So we left, and I forgot so many things about her, my sister. I forgot the house too, we all did. I visited once, but that was maybe twenty years ago, maybe more. I haven't been reminded of her in so long—'

Radhamohan was staring at the sepia-faded girl in the album, memories of evening conversations with her in the balcony suddenly vivid in his mind.

'And her name?' he asked slowly.

'Her name was Lokkhi.'

A Small Statue

Prattatatva

I HEARD THIS story from my friend Sukumar babu.

Those who know about Indian history and archeology will have heard of Sukumar Sen. He was a valuable member of the government of India's Archeological Survey for a long time, and a part of the team that led the Patna excavations under Dr Spooner. He was, for a while, a curator in the archeological division of the Indian Museum, and specialized in Buddhist statues. Apart from his two best known books, *Pre-Gupta Art* and *A Treatise on Indian Iconography*, he has written several journal and popular culture articles on his area of expertise.

The room that he uses as a study bears witness to his deep interest in the history of India. It is so overfull of broken bits of ancient brick, old cotton-paper manuscripts with splintered wooden spines, piles of palm-leaf scrolls, and statues of various excavated gods and goddesses, that there is barely any place to put your feet down in the room, should you happen to visit him. His particular interest is in the statues, and he spends hours of work classifying and labelling these.

When he receives an item from an archaeological dig, he first spends a lot of time examining it minutely with a magnifying glass. Then he turns to the books and manuscripts in his collection to cross-reference the piece, to understand where it comes from historically, and what it may mean in that context. Then he will put a label on it saying something like 'Buddhamurti, Tara'. However, such a non-specific label is not usually to his satisfaction. You can hear him talk to himself while poring over books and papers—'Hm, this seems to be from the Lalitgiri dig, so maybe it's not a Tara, what can it be?' The big magnifying glass comes out again, and the small statue is examined closely from every angle. The statue has an arm broken off, he examines that area with particular attention, and the absorbed murmuring begins once more—'I think there was a lotus in that hand, yes, perhaps that's correct, let me see—' and then he will carefully remove his previous label from the statue, and attach a new one, saying something like 'Buddhamurti Jombola'.

I used to watch Dr Sen behave in this persnickety manner for hours, and since I did not understand it at all, it would amuse me. I was not the only one who found this extreme absorption a little strange. People who understood the area of study better than me would shake their heads and remark on his extravagant devotion to his work. The common understanding of Dr Sen was that he had turned what was merely an interesting career into a mission for life, and that this was both excessive and unnecessary. But I was very fond of Dr Sen and his eccentricities, and I would go to see him as often as I could.

That afternoon, Sukumarbabu was immersed in a book about the disciplinary practices of the Sen dynasty, when I showed up like a people's revolution to destroy the scholarly tranquility of his study. To his credit, he was very happy to see me. Once I had poured my day's banal irritations out to him, as I frequently did, I realised that he seemed preoccupied with something else, something he had not yet brought up in our conversation. He got up abruptly and said, 'Let me ask for tea, then listen. I have a story to tell you. I have been wanting to tell this story for a while—I don't know why it feels as if this story needs to be told now.'

It was a cold, damp day outside. Sukumarbabu shut the door and sat back down again. The tea came, steaming hot and comforting. As we sipped the tea, he started with his story.

***

'You must have heard of the old archaeological dig sites at Bikrampur? It is difficult to pinpoint the age of some of the artefacts found at those sites. We have known some of the outer parts of that site to look exactly the way they seem now—just undefined heaps on the ground—for a very long time. Based on the incomplete information we have, dating several of those structures exactly has proved impossible.

Some time ago, the Dhaka Museum became interested in a more complete excavation of a part of the outer reaches of that site. Before the Museum, both the Barendra Investigation Society and the Dhaka Literary Association had called for further excavations there. I had turned down that project, since I believed that the benefit from a fuller investigation into the site would be greatly overshadowed by the expenses and commitment required for the dig. This time however, the Dhaka Museum was willing to provide the resources, and adamant that Bikrampur needed more complete excavation. Approached directly by the Museum, which could not be denied, I reluctantly agreed to head this archaeological project.

On reaching the site, I saw that there was not one, but two hillocks in the area marked for the dig. Very close by was an extensive, but shallow lake which was almost dry at that time of the year. Both hillocks were quite large, and overgrown with thorn bushes. The one towards the west had been made almost impenetrable by dense, spiky overgrowth. The one to the east was slightly smaller, and it had a section towards the back which was relatively free of thorn bushes. It was from this area that we decided to start our slow dive into the eastern hill.

Archaeological excavations usually begin with a tentative pre-set plan based on any information that may already be available about the site. Once the digging begins, this plan is slowly and carefully revised in sections. The kinds of revisions to the original plan are based partly on ongoing discoveries from the site, and partly on informed guesswork by the experts working on the dig. This gradually unfolding methodology had worked very well for the massive Patna excavations. However, this is a complex process and needs a large scale and several experts to carry out properly. I did not see a need to follow such a detailed process in small local rural dig. We did not have any experts from the Archaeological Society on this little team, except myself. This was because the dig was being handled by the Dhaka PWD.

We had heard the local legends surrounding these hillocks. The larger one was called the Hill of the Agnostic Scholar, supposedly after a learned local man who lived nearby and had deserted the Vaishnavite faith. He was reputedly mistrusted by the locals of the time because he abandoned his faith. Others said that this supposedly agnostic individual had never come anywhere near these hillocks, or indeed the entire larger area.'

Here, Sukumarbabu paused and looked straight at me, 'But I know who had spent time near those barrows, who had lived there. I suspect there are others whose research led to the same conclusions that I have reached. But they had no proof, so they did not talk about it.

I have a kind of proof, but I cannot talk about it. I think you will understand my long silence when you hear how I know about the history of this area.'

'But anyway, back to the Bikrampur excavation. Work proceeded slowly. The thorn bushes had to be cut back with much pain before the digging began. Mr K, a representative from the Dhaka Museum, attended the dig full-time. Like me, archaeology was not just his profession, but also his chosen vocation. It was his deep interest and enthusiasm that had led to the dig being sanctioned by the Museum, and his persuasive abilities that had brought me here. Picture this—Mr K sitting on a camp chair under a huge neem tree, staring fixedly at the dig from morning to evening, every single day. He had such hope in his eyes. I remember looking at my friend radiating anticipation toward those hillocks for days on end, and thinking that nothing less than an ancient royal palace emerging from the ground would satisfy him. Perhaps he would settle for a hitherto entirely unknown history of Bengal written on a palm-leaf scroll? No, probably the find would have to be as significant as the undamaged mummified body of the Agnostic Scholar himself. I feared that Mr K would be quite dissatisfied by the results of the dig, and this worried me periodically.

The first thing we found in the ground was an intact mud jar. It was clearly ancient. We had no way to date it exactly, but it was clear that jars of this particular design were no longer made anywhere that we knew of.

The curve from the neck of the jar to its base was so beautiful, and so flawlessly wrought, that we thought it was probably the work of a master artisan. If the creator had been a village potter, he must have been highly respected in his time.

The jar was half-full of cowrie shells, which we knew were in use as currency a long time ago. Some bygone householder would have stored the shells away as insurance against future uncertainties. The future he was shoring up against had long come and gone, and the little hoard had never been recovered and used.

Over the next few weeks, many more artefacts emerged from the barrows—pieces of broken earthen pots, jars, bowls and basins, a completely rusted sword, a lamp, many pieces of ancient brick and, last of all, a small statue of a goddess in black stone. It is this statue that is at the centre of my story.

It was found from deep inside the smaller hill. Made of the kind of black granite that is now mostly quarried from Rajmahal in Jharkhand, it was surprisingly undamaged for an object that had been buried under the earth for a long time. We could see that the statue had no nicks or breaks even when it was freshly excavated, with earth still clinging to it. But once the mud was wiped off, we realised how beautifully finished the little statue actually was. It shone with a lustre rarely seen in stone that has not been freshly polished, and every detail of the carving was clear to the naked eye. If we did not know that it was possibly a few thousand years old and had just been taken from the excavation in front of our eyes, we could be forgiven for thinking that it had been created quite recently.

The goddess was Saraswati, but she had several prominent elements of Buddhist style in the carving. If she did not have the veena in her hand that marked her as unmistakably Saraswati, the other features of the statue could well have led to categorizing her as not the Hindu goddess Saraswati, but the Bodhisattva, or Buddha-aspect, Manjushree.

The statue was taken away from us to be properly cleaned by some of the younger members of the dig. When it was returned, I took one look at it and rose from my chair as if propelled by some invisible force. I had seen many statues of many kinds in my long career as a professional archaeologist. I specialized in them. But this one was dazzling, almost unbelievable in the realism of the figure of the goddess. It was difficult to believe that a human being had carved the smile blossoming on her beautiful face. The face itself—strange as it may be to say this about a statuette made of black stone—looked as if it was real, and made of skin and muscle and bone. The entire figure, every contour of the body, the way the hands and feet were carved, the fingers resting on the veena, was flawless. Every one of those elegantly tapering fingers, every fold of cloth seemed as if it may move at any time. I stared at the little statue dumbfounded, unbelieving at the sheer skill of the craftsmanship which had created this exquisite piece of beauty, and unbelieving of my instinctive, uncontrolled and purely emotional reaction to it.

Once the dig was over, I returned home and placed the beautiful little statue on a shelf with my collection of meditating Buddhas. I would look at it every morning almost as an act of devotion. I have never been an imaginative man, but it seemed to me that her fascinating almond-shaped eyes smiled a little more every day, that they grew brighter and more life-like when I saw them each passing morning. I am not exaggerating when I say that I had never before seen an object of stone that was anything like that statue.

In the meanwhile, I continued my efforts to date the statue as accurately as possible. The problem was that nothing the excavation had thrown up made this task easier. It was clear from some of the stylistic features that the statue was from a Pre-Gupta period, and also that it had been carved by a master craftsman in the eastern, rather than western part of Bengal. The latter was easily deduced from a small stylized umbrella-form over the head of the goddess. I had seen such forms in other statues carved in eastern Bengal, so this, at least, seemed to be a reasonable conclusion.

One particular Sunday during this time, I spent a contented evening playing some rounds of chess with a neighbour, came back home, and retired early.'

Sukumarbabu paused, and frowned a little. Then he continued, clearly somewhat worried. 'Please know that I am able to speak of what I will now, only because it is you who is listening. I have not told this to anyone else, because I suspect no one else will believe me.

'It was not clear how long I slept, but my sleep was broken for no apparent reason. The first thing I remember was the fragrance. There was an overwhelming and very lovely scent in my room. It smelled of mingled incense, flowers, ghee and sandalwood, like the inner sanctum of a temple while prayers are being offered. My half-awake consciousness wrapped around the fragrance as if intoxicated. I had no idea what time it was, since the clock was on the wall above my head, ticking away.

The dark seemed to lighten as my eyes adjusted. As this happened, I saw a figure standing in the middle of the room, close to my bed. His head was shaved, his clothes were that of a Buddhist monk. His face and arms, not covered by the robe he wore, were glowing as if he was illuminated from within. Still a little blurry from deep sleep, I struggled to focus on this astonishing vision. But it disappeared before I could pull myself properly to the surface.

Unsettled by the quick succession of very unusual events, I bolted upright on my bed and turned to look at the clock. It was two o'clock in the morning, and an incoherence must have taken hold of me, because all I could think of at that moment was the story of Abu Ben Adhem that I had heard in my childhood ("May his tribe increase").

It was impossible to lie down for a little while. But I gradually soothed myself into believing that the vision of the Buddhist monk was just an extraordinarily vivid dream, and that I needed to get some more hours of rest before daybreak. This self-calming worked quite well. I lay down again, and sleep came easier than I had thought it would.

The next time I awoke, it was with a start. There it was again, the intoxicating fragrance in my room. This time, the fragrance seemed to permeate my being and take possession of every sense. It wrapped itself around my consciousness and forced me to look up, towards the rest of the room. And there he was again, the illuminated Buddhist monk, standing beside my bed and looking at me.

As I looked at him, the room seemed to melt away, even from the edges of my perception. I saw a city, resplendent with large open spaces and old trees dense with foliage, casting luxuriant shade on the ground under them. The city had so many beautiful houses, and porticos wrapped in shining marble. There were grand courtyards, and soaring domes. All the buildings I could see were remarkable in the elegance and grace of their symmetry. The place seemed inhabited almost entirely by Buddhist monks, going about their work and leisure. The houses were populated by those who seemed to be students, bent over studying, or otherwise handling books and manuscripts.

There was a particularly beautiful tree that caught my eye. It was a magnificent peepul tree in full bloom, but with red leaves. Under it was a platform made of the finest white marble, on which several students were seated cross-legged. The Buddhist monk present at my bedside was also seated under the tree, in fact he seemed to be the teacher. As I watched, wonderstruck, red leaves showered off the tree onto the students and teacher underneath. It felt as if the tree itself was blessing the learning in progress beneath its lush, protective canopy.

The scene melted away. I started hearing the mingled sounds of all kinds of musical instruments. It seemed that I was now in the middle of some kind of large-scale celebration. Around me were throngs of happy men and women dressed in their festive best. The people in the carvings at the Ajanta caves seemed to have stepped off the wall and into this joyous occasion. Their clothing and manners were not of the current times, they felt ancient, timeless, undateable. On the fringes of the celebration were a large number of strong-looking soldiers standing loosely at attention, dressed in ceremonial armour that had been buffed and polished till it shone. Beside them stood their gorgeous warhorses, also dressed in ceremonial array. Only the horses looked impatient with the festivities, occasionally pawing the ground and snorting restlessly. Being at rest and peace did not appear to suit these magnificent animals.

At the centre of this vast celebration stood three figures. The beautiful young woman in red, resplendent with jewellery and flowers was clearly the bride. Her soon-to-be husband, a tall, handsome, strong-looking man, with the transparent face of youth, wore a shining steel armour which glinted in the light. His warlike attire was relieved only by a garland of flowers, similar to the ones the bride wore. I had clearly arrived at a significant point in the marriage ceremony. As I watched, the third person at the centre of the event took the lovely young woman's hand, and put it carefully in the hand of the godlike young man. This third figure looked familiar, so I looked closer. He was the Buddhist monk I had already met.

The wedding vanished. I was suddenly cold, so cold. My teeth started to chatter, my toes went icy and numb. Spread out around me as far as the eye could reach in any direction was a frozen world of bone-chilling frost. Snow was storming over this desolate landscape. Even through the driving blizzard, I could faintly make out that the horizon all around was made of the tops of very tall peaks and ridges. I was somewhere high in the mountains, on a narrow path that wound its way through the rugged, snow-blanketed landscape. A strong-looking Buddhist monk was walking the path ahead of me, weaving precariously, and coming close to failing sometimes. His head would drop to his chest and his gait would almost come to a standstill, but he kept pushing forward. It seemed that only willpower was keeping him going.

Somewhere far ahead, well beyond the snowstorm that surrounded us, a setting sun lit up the high peaks. It touched only the tops of the mountains and turned them blood-red. To my frozen mind, it looked as if the demons of that high world had fired huge torches, and that the red fire of those torches was the only source of light in that forsaken white kingdom of ice and storm.

The snowstorm grew in severity, and erased everything around me. I could no longer see anything but featureless blinding dense white.

When the veil lifted, the surroundings felt gentler and softer, more gratefully familiar. I found myself in rural Bengal. There was a humble cottage with a roof of straw, and a dense bamboo thicket behind it. The shade was deep and cool under bamboo leaves rustling softly in the breeze. Birds were twittering from inside the grove, hopping around in the sunlit greenery. A young man, just only past his teenage years, was sitting on the low packed-earth porch of the cottage. In front of him was a known object. I looked closer. It was definitely the beautiful statue we had excavated at Bikrampur, the one that was now among the collection of meditating Buddhas in my study. The young man was gazing at the statue with an expression of mingled devotion, awe and love—as if it marked a long-time desire fulfilled, a wish that he could not quite believe had come true. It seemed strangely appropriate that this young man's intense, longing eyes should be fixed with such love on this exquisite statue, under the clouded late-evening skies of ancient rural Bengal.

This vision passed too. Now, I was back on my bed in my room, and the luminous, and now familiar Buddhist monk was still at my bedside. He spoke, for the first time. I paid spellbound attention to everything he said, so I remember it in the smallest detail. This is what he said—

"The statue you dug out of the ground has pulled me back to this world, after a very long time. I was a flesh and blood man just like you, but that was almost a thousand years ago. My home stood on the ground from which you found the statue.

"You have spent your life in the pursuit of knowledge—that is why it is possible for me to come here and show myself to you. That is also why it brings me so much joy to show you glimpses of my life, aspects that you would not know by simply studying the statue you found.

"I am Dipankar. During the reign of the king Nayapala, I was among the seniormost teachers at the great university of Nalanda. Before that, I was a teacher at the village in which I was born. But I heard the great Buddha speak, and his words changed my life. Leaving behind my family, my land, and the religion of my birth, I went to Nalanda. Thereafter, they did not like me very much in my homeland. I heard that they called me the agnostic scholar, because I had forsaken my family's religion.

"When the Buddha's gentle teachings were abandoned in favour of discord and violence in Tibet, I followed the great sage Shakyashree to those cold mountains to try and save the love preached in my chosen faith. You have seen part of that difficult journey.

"You have also seen a day of another kind, one of great joy to me. When the Chedi king Karna set out to conquer as large a territory as he could, the only ruler powerful enough to stop his victorious rampage through central India was my king Nayapala, the ruler of Gaur, Magadh and Bengal. I was having a usual day of teaching at Nalanda the day Karna had to arrive at an understanding of peace with Nayapala. What a day of rejoicing that became as the news came in! Nobody slept even as it got darker, there were celebrations on the streets all night. I remember that day as if it was yesterday.

"A few days after this treaty, Karna's daughter Jaubanasree was married to Nayapala's son Vigrahapal III, who was next in line for succession. To my great joy, I was asked to officiate at that wedding. You have seen that happy day too.

"When I was very young, I learned to work in stone from a skilled craftsman who lived in our village. As I grew older, and my life became more complicated, I always tried my best to keep those early skills polished and updated. But you have seen my best work in statue-making, the one piece into which I poured everything I had ever learned about working in stone. It is with you now. I was very pleased with my image of Saraswati. I was so attached to her that she held the power to bring me back to this world, as she has done now.

"I left the statue in the land I was born, but they did not like me there. Not only had I become a Buddhist, but the way I adopted and practiced Buddhism was not like a religion the way they saw it. I considered myself at war with ignorance, wherever it existed, wherever it could do harm. This made it difficult for people to see me as just a Buddhist monk belonging to the Buddhist faith, and this annoyed them, it made them uncomfortable. But I am only one of such people who battle darkness, wherever it may be. There have been others, and there will be more. You are one of them, which is why I am able to appear to you, to talk to you. May you continue to fight the dark, and may you continue to win."

The monk Dipankar slowly disappeared from my bedside. I must have fallen asleep, because the next time I awoke it was to late morning light, and I could hear someone sweeping the verandah in front of my room.'

***

His story done, Dr Sen looked at me quietly, as if to gauge my reaction. 'Where is the statue now?' I asked.

'At the Dhaka Museum,' he said. 'You can go and see it anytime you like.'

Acknowledgements

THIS BOOK WOULD not have been possible without Ajitha GS, who patiently heard me plan to work on ghost stories for years, read some terrible first attempts at supernatural translation, told me what I needed to fix, and guided me gently to Kanishka Gupta. Kanishka's certainty that he could find a place for this book has been an unfailing source of encouragement, thanks for that, K! Many thanks are due to Renuka Chatterjee and the team at Speaking Tiger for being that welcoming space for this book. Much gratitude to Prachi Sharma for her sensitive edit of the manuscript.

A big thank you to Arunava Sinha, who helped me understand the project of this sort of translation, and answered some essential questions, so ensuring that the translations proceeded. Thank you to Bibhutibhushan's grandson, Trinankur Banerjee, for assuring me that I was getting 'the tone right', when I sent him anxious drafts of the translations. Many thanks to Baidik Bhattacharya for his insights into the writings of Bibhutibhushan in Bengali, when I was floundering with making connections with his larger body of work.

Formative thanks to my father, Basudev Mookerjee, from whom my interest in the supernatural began. He saw ghosts on at least two occasions, and told those stories in a manner that became indelibly etched on my much younger brain. Sujoy Chakravarty, for his unfailing capacity to believe that I can do pretty much anything to which I set my mind, for teaching me to play bass while I worked on this volume (because, 'the E minor is a truly ominous chord'), and for so much else, spanning a quarter-century. Abhijit Gupta (Tintin) for the gift of the volume from which I translated these stories, and for the co-journey of the Jadavpur University Press. Big thanks for being the best boss and friend in the world, as well as a heck of a publisher. Huge thanks to the team at the JUP, where kindness is a way of work. I'm so grateful to be part of the team.

My superwoman-sisters, Rimi B. Chatterjee, Prachi Deshpande, Sanjukta Roy, Oyndrila Sarkar, Jenny Jose, Sohini Sengupta, Sunandini Banerjee, Kajori Aikat, Sashwati Banerjee, Proma Basu Roy, Marakah Mancini, Nabanita Sarkar and Priyanka Verma, for knowledge, ideas, pow-wow, clear-thinking, support, encouragement, ass-kicking, feedback, corrective lectures, anchoring, and so many other important micro things that make up women's relationships with each other. Mandakini Gupta for the incredible confectionery whenever I fail and feel like falling on my face. I learn all the time from my superwoman-sisters, and more gratitude is owed to each of them than they know.

Bibek Bhattacharya has told me stories of the uncanny in art, scripture and architecture for years now, sometimes with pictures. I owe him for keeping my supernatural imagination ablaze and running. Priyodorshi Banerjee, Sandeep Banerjee, and Arijit Sen for myriad on-the-spot readings of the world, feedback on my ideas and writing, and years of friendship and encouragement. Suhrid Shankar Chattopadhyay and Rudraneil Sengupta, for demonstrations of how brutal reality can be woven into compelling narrative. Rohan Ganguli, Sayatya Mallick, and Atandra Chakraborty, for riffs that rang as soundtrack in my head in the feverish early summer mornings of translation, and so much knowledge about sound, and silence, that my mental filing cabinets are creaking. Big thanks are due to Shubhabrata Roy, for hope for the future.

My teachers at Jadavpur University—Sajni Mukherji, Sukanta Chaudhuri, Supriya Chaudhuri, and Ananda Lal, first guides to the power of narrative. It has been an honour, and a pleasure, to be back at JU, and to work with them in recent years. Two decades of thanks are due to Mohan Dutta, social scientist and advisor extraordinaire, who will always be in my head, telling me to look at details, voices, experience, and equations of power, in narratives of life. Those lessons have rung true through the years, as I was reminded while working on this volume.

Immeasurable thanks are due to Sunandini Banerjee for the lush, psychedelic, fever dream cover, that perfectly encapsulates the atmosphere of the book.

And finally, my furry girls and boys—the late Bibi Rani, Patchgirl, Rugboi, Vacuum Cleaner aka Bonolota, Toffi, Maya, and Sridevi, for making each day a six-dog day.

I hope that all the humans thanked here enjoy the book. I hope that you enjoy this book too.